Flight

A Gay Fairy Tale

Leta Blake

Prologue

"ONCE UPON A time, in a castle by a great, foamy sea, there lived a kind-hearted king and his beautiful queen." Mateo knelt on the dirt floor of the castle's dovecote, surrounded by the children of servants. The doves cooed and swooped, and a few of the older boys ducked their heads, but the youngest were far too rapt to take much notice.

"In sets of two and three, the queen gave birth to eleven girls, each more beautiful than the last, and finally to one handsome, healthy boy."

"Does that mean you think Princess Luz

is the prettiest, sir?" a tall, dark boy interrupted.

"*Silencio*. I'm telling a story. Are you looking to get me into trouble with my sisters?"

Mateo was accustomed to being accosted by the children during his walk from the castle to the dovecote. He was known for spinning a good yarn, and he'd long made himself available to the young ones of the kingdom in a way he generally refrained from with the adults. Unlike unscrupulous courtiers, the children never asked for favors greater than an apple or another tale.

In some ways, he thought of himself as more like them than not. He was young and didn't yet suffer from the heavy weight of many courtly responsibilities. Just last month his sister Blanca had gone so far as to pinch his cheeks before the knights. It had been humiliating, if rather expected. A knot of frustration grew in the pit of his stomach. He and Luz had come of age several weeks past, so no matter how young at heart he might be, his family should treat him accordingly.

"More, sir?" a quiet, shy one asked, her eyes bright with hope.

Mateo had planned to spend the morning working with his doves, and he hoped to send the children away sooner rather than later, but how could he refuse such a face?

"Of course, naturally, all the king's children were vibrant, intelligent and sometimes mischievous creatures."

The children all laughed and tittered at his description of himself and his sisters, but Mateo spoke the truth. While he thought his own appearance was pleasant enough, what with his dark, curly hair, warm brown eyes, fit form and an eye for fashion—his sisters were in truth remarkably beautiful and much sought after despite their wayward tendencies.

"Laugh all you like, but the king loved them all with every beat of his heart." Mateo tried in vain to keep his mind from the fact that his father's heart was old and failing now. "And as the prince and princesses grew, the king and queen agreed theirs was a charmed life."

Mateo glanced up at the doves that seemed to be listening along. One of them cooed, and Mateo sighed. No good story came without sadness—not even his own.

"The king and queen also knew that like all beautiful things, it was too good to last." The children's gazes fell to the ground, for the whole kingdom had suffered the loss. "One dark day their fears came true. Fever ravaged the court. But the kingdom was lucky. Only one was lost. The queen fought bravely, but in the end she left the kind-hearted king and their handsome children behind."

There were other, far more pleasing and fantastical stories Mateo could tell about lands of fae, and nights of dancing, stories passed on to him and his sisters from their old nurse, but he often found himself telling this sad, all-too-true story instead. In some way it gave him comfort.

"After the queen's passing, the king became even more attached to his outrageously handsome son," here Mateo stopped and feigned arrogance, "and his eleven astoundingly gorgeous daughters."

The young ones laughed again, and Mateo continued. "He hated to let his children out of his sight, chafing even when they ventured into the village or the seaside. He worried terribly any time the princesses and prince left the castle itself, pleading with them to stay at his side. Despite the many suitors requesting their hands, the king always refused, much preferring to keep his children near him than to suffer the loss of their company."

Mateo smiled a little bitterly at this. The only people who had ever talked to his father about asking for his hand once he came of age had not been to his liking. The first had been an older, widowed king who, having found through the years that his taste ran in such a manner, hoped to start a new life with a young, handsome prince of the same persuasion. The second was a princess that Mateo believed was actually much more interested in his sister Adelita, but everyone knew Adelita's tastes did not run that way, given how she flirted with the knights.

Mateo's wants and needs had been little considered by either contender for his hand, so when his father refused on his behalf without even consulting him, Mateo had felt only relief. As a child, he'd dreamed of one day meeting a man who cared for him and for whom he felt admiration and love in return. But time passed, and stifled as he and his sisters were by their father's affection, Mateo no longer looked to love and marriage as a path to freedom and happiness. Rather he saw any such commitment as a smothering restriction at worst and a recipe for crushing grief at best.

Mateo sought instead a man for whom

he might feel a mild affection or an enchanting affinity, and with whom he might slake the natural desire burning in his loins. For now, he was content to indulge in heated fantasies featuring one or two of the most attractive of the knights. The king and his people did not care if he married a man or a woman, so long as the marriage benefitted the kingdom.

His sisters were another matter. They had become so restless that the oldest set of triplets especially argued for their father to let them go to a husband—or a wife, in the case of Herminia. Or even to go beyond the castle's walls. Mateo could not blame them, for he yearned to spread his own wings. Yet of late, all such complaints had halted utterly. Mateo frowned, thinking of his sisters' mysterious behavior.

As if summoned by his thoughts, a voice, worn and ragged, cried out, "Mateo!" The children all stared, likely wondering who would dare to address their prince by his first name.

"Lámina," Mateo said softly, rising from his crouch to better see his old nurse above the heads of the children. She was barely as tall as the oldest of the bunch, her fuzzy hair looking thinner than ever, and her skirts muddy from her dash across the wet yard. She was panting, eyes wide, and held her hand over her heart. He feared she might collapse. "What's the matter?"

"Sir, your father." Lámina paused to catch her breath.

Mateo's heart wrenched. His father had so many spells of late. Had he collapsed? Was he all right?

Lámina alleviated his greatest fears. "He's quite angry. You should go to him immediately."

Mateo left the telling of the story, the doves and the children behind, knowing even as he raced toward the castle and into his father's court just what the crisis would be.

"YOU *WILL* TELL me where you've been going. You cannot deceive me with sweet looks and lies." The king's face was red and his second chin wobbled with righteous anger. His long red robes glowed in the sunlight streaming in from the windows overhead, and his finger shook as he pointed it at each offender one by one.

Mateo skirted around the edges of the room, moving through the dark recesses beneath the columns, pushing past courtiers, who watched and listened avidly. When Mateo finally stepped into the open area before his father's dais, he saw his eleven sisters standing in a line before the throne, dressed hastily in unkempt clothes, their hair still tied into braids for sleeping. On the floor before them, their slippers rested soles up, revealing holes worn all the way through each pair. Mateo walked past, pausing only to try to catch Luz's eye for some kind of explanation. Finally, he stood next to his father and put a hand on his unsteady shoulder. Despite his father's health and advanced years, Mateo suspected pure rage caused the tremors.

"These slippers were given to you new yesterday morning. And this is not the first time, my daughters. Every morning for two weeks you say that you go nowhere, that you do nothing, and yet look! Explain these holes. They do not come from 'nowhere' and 'nothing'." He smacked his palm against the arm of his throne.

Mateo squeezed his shoulder. "Calm, Papá."

"Papá, we have slept in our beds every night," said Adelita, the eldest and their father's favorite. She appeared a bit ragged around the edges—though somehow still vibrant—as she bowed her dark head and lowered her eyes. "We swear it."

"Yes Papá, we swear it," Blanca echoed.

She was born fourteen minutes after Adelita, and her usually white cheeks were as flushed as hot-pink roses. Her eyes glowed with the obvious lie.

"Catalina," the king addressed the third of the eldest triplets, born ten minutes after Blanca. "You have always been a steadying influence on your siblings, a mother to the younger ones and a friend to the older. But now it seems you're an accomplice. You bring me shame. Redeem yourself and answer your father with the truth."

"Papá," Catalina said softly, her hands trembling along with her voice. "Please, Papá."

"Answer."

"Every night. We, all of us. We go."

The king leaned forward in anticipation of his most dependable daughter uttering the answer to his very simple question. Mateo waited too, certain that Catalina—who had never been able to tell a lie—would confess their sins. He watched his sisters squirm under their father's gaze.

"We go to sleep. In our beds. Where we remain until morning, Papá," Catalina said, lifting her chin to meet his gaze with a defiant eye.

Down the line the king went, questioning them all as Mateo silently watched. The second set of triplets—Delfina, Elisa and Felipa—and the quadruplets—Gracia, Herminia, Imelda, Josefina—and finally his twin sister Luz all insisted they'd spent the night in their beds.

"Every evening for the last two weeks you lock us in and put guards at the doors, Papá," Luz said, tension crackling in the air. She met Mateo's eye and added with a bit more shame on her face, "How could we go anywhere?"

"Yes, Father," Imelda said. She folded her arms over her chest and growled. "We don't know what happens to our shoes. Perhaps the fairies borrow them to dance."

A titter went through the court, and

Mateo glanced toward Lámina, who had staggered in looking sweaty and on the verge of death. Lámina's fairy stories had been their nightly fare as they grew up and had no doubt inspired Imelda's comment.

"Please, Papá dear, may we be excused?" Herminia asked sweetly, obviously hoping to soften her sister's impertinence.

"What more do you want from us?" Imelda said. The other sisters shot her a warning look. "We've told you all we know."

"What more do I want?" The king's voice was so loud the doors rattled at the back of the room and every person within flinched, covering their ears with their hands. "The truth."

The king turned to Mateo then, his rheumy eyes burning with hot rage. "Mateo, you and Luz have always been thick as thieves. Do you have nothing to add to this conversation?"

"No, Father," Mateo answered, his eyes focused on his twin sister's face. If only he did. The king had only been the best father, gentle, kind, loving—if overly possessive and too protective by half—and it saddened Mateo to see his sisters deceiving him thus.

The king rose. "So be it. Let it be known!"

Each ear in the room turned to the king, awaiting his proclamation. Mateo saw the hopeful brightness in each eye, and noted which courtiers stepped forth from the dark shadows in anticipation of whatever drama was about to unfold before them.

"No matter how they come about the information, whatsoever man or woman can tell me where my daughters go at night, and what they do to leave their shoes in such a state, will be rewarded with a residence befitting royalty, horses and household servants."

The crowd murmured, eager voices rising until the king silenced them with a glare and continued.

"And a chance as heir to my throne with

the choice of any of my children to take as wife or husband."

In the stunned hush, Mateo watched his sisters' faces, seeing panic flash through them as they understood the implication of their father's decree. Then he realized with a twist of his gut that his own fate had also been offered up to whatever rogue might manage to solve the puzzle.

"The prince too, sire?" a voice called out.

"Indeed," the king answered.

Heat surged through Mateo—anger mixed with adamant rejection of his predicament. It wasn't fair!

The king looked about, clearly anticipating that someone would come forward with information now that a general pardon had been given and such an extravagant reward offered. Mateo half expected one of his sisters to finally betray the others, perhaps by bargaining for the rights to her own hand. But their claim to innocence held fast. No sister stepped forward.

Mateo's eyes fell on Sir Franco, a knight whose strong shoulders and arms had featured prominently in Mateo's midnight fantasies. He held his breath, hoping Franco might take up the challenge, even though the man's tastes ran invariably toward women. But alas, Sir Franco turned to move deeper into the shadows. Mateo didn't know if he was relieved or disappointed.

The king gritted his teeth. "Leave me. All of you. Girls, retire to your room and remain there." To Mateo's surprise, none of his sisters moaned or wept about their confinement, but instead scampered off as though they could think of no better place than their chambers to spend the rest of their days.

Alone on the dais after his father exited as well, Mateo was immediately set upon by the courtiers, all with questions about his sisters—did he know where they went, did he have any ideas? Mateo knew that it was only a matter of time before one or more of them took up the gauntlet and tried for his father's proffered reward.

When the distinct sound of the court messengers trumpeting the king's proclamation to the village reached him, Mateo finally broke free from the insipid courtiers—none of them Sir Franco, which he decided was not disappointing. He was a grown man now and didn't need a knight to fight his battles for him. He had to convince his sisters to reveal their secret or find a manner to discover it himself. With steps fueled by determination, Mateo returned to the dovecote to feed his birds and create a plan.

Chapter One

A FTER THE KING'S proclamation, more than two hundred people from all walks of life—soldiers, tailors, princes, countesses and thieves—had come forward to try for the prize. None were turned away. As arguments broke out, a proper list was made and a procedure established.

With the caveat that any impropriety would be severely punished—and none would dare lay a finger on the princesses and enrage the king further—each fortune seeker was allowed three nights in the sisters' chambers. Then if they could provide no answer as to the girls' activities, the king moved on to the next in the long line of chancers.

So far, three men and two women had entered the sisters' chambers confident of their ability to penetrate their veil of secrets, only to fall asleep, night after night. They woke in the mornings to find the princesses, all pink cheeks and smiles, tucked in their beds—and their slippers worn through.

Of course Mateo had confronted his sisters himself, starting with Luz, but that conversation had gotten him nowhere.

"Don't you see what you're costing Papá with your games? There are murmurs in the court that if he cannot control even his own daughters, how can he rule? Own the truth, Luz. What can be the worst of it?"

Luz had merely tossed her dark head, lifted her shoulders in an elegant shrug, and walked away as if he were nothing more than an annoying bee buzzing about her head. He'd seen that gesture from his other sisters his entire life, but it was the first time from his twin. She hadn't even bothered to look remorseful.

It had gone no better with the older ones. They'd laughed at him outright, cooed, clucked and spoken to him as if he was still a child. He'd been lucky to escape their clutches with only a few flowers braided into his hair. *That* had certainly pleased the giggling servant children he'd passed on the way to the dovecote. At least Pura, his favorite dove, had plucked the blossoms from his hair and absconded with them to her nest, using her beak to twist prettiness out of his humiliation.

After the fifth fortune seeker had failed, on a day when the king was discouraged, angry and thundering with threats of taking a harsher course with his daughters, the same widowed king who'd once made the unsuccessful bid for Mateo's hand stepped up to take his chance.

"I, Rey Hernando, do hereby declare my intent to discover what mischief the princesses commit. I ask as the prize for my certain triumph only the hand of Prince Mateo. For I have riches, lands and servants already—all of which I am only too happy to share with your son, good king. I require only his companionship, kindness and his sweet love to warm my bed."

Hearing the murmur of the courtiers, and knowing full well the pictures King Hernando's words brought to their minds, Mateo's skin prickled with hot embarrassment. He had no choice but to smile politely upon the stooped man's grizzled face. He'd expected to be Hernando's choice, of course, but having it announced so baldly to the court was humiliating. The very idea of being beneath someone so old—or, depending on King Hernando's inclination, on top for that matter—made his stomach roil.

When King Hernando smiled at him, licking his mustached mouth with a red, wet tongue, Mateo wished for the first time since the whole business began that his sisters would continue to outwit them all—if only for three more nights.

King Hernando arrogantly outlined his plan for success. He'd brought with him a giant bell and six men. These men would stand outside the sisters' chambers, taking turns banging upon the bell every few minutes, ensuring that King Hernando would stay awake the entire night. At Mateo's father's request, the men demonstrated the power of the bell.

An hour later, Mateo's head still rang with the noise. He had to admit that King Hernando stood the best chance of anyone so far of discovering his sisters' secret.

Unfortunately, he was no closer to discovering it himself.

"WHY DO THEY rebel in such ways, Lámina?" Mateo asked as he followed her through her herb garden, watching her bend low to pull a weed, then stoop to snap off a branch of rosemary.

She made a noise that offered little information about her opinion.

"It's not as if they are bad girls. Well, Catalina is a good girl. They are all good girls," Mateo said.

When Lámina cleared her throat, Mateo laughed and amended, "Except for Adelita and Blanca and Delfina and Herminia and Imelda and Josefina. They're a bit of trouble sometimes."

"And you are no trouble at all," she countered.

"I don't make problems as they do."

Lámina shrugged. "Trouble is many things. Sometimes trouble is refusing the hands of old men and princesses when it is your duty to accept." She glanced up at him, shielding her eyes from the sun. Her smile was crooked and revealed brown teeth. "Old Lámina sees how it is with you."

Certainly, he'd come to seek her advice, but he'd given away nothing of his plan—or lack thereof—yet. "It's rather like being sold," Mateo said, kicking at a clod of dirt.

"Is it now?" she murmured, returning her focus to her plants.

"Indeed. Only, instead of being sent along to the highest bidder, I am a prize to be won by the first to outwit eleven mischievous girls."

"I believe they are women, *mi pájaro*."

Mateo sighed. Of course they were women. They were women who should have, by all accounts, been married with families of their own. If they had all been settled, their antics would not be Papá's problem. Mateo doubted—if they were properly matched—they'd even have time for mischief amidst their wifely duties.

"They should be married," Lámina said, her voice raspy and quiet. "As should you. You are a man grown and proud."

Mateo's head snapped up. It was not the

first time Lámina had expressed such a sentiment about his sisters, but it was the first she'd mentioned anything at all about his uncoupled state.

"Leaving me aside, I agree."

"Why leaving you aside? Is there someone particular you would choose? Sir Franco? Old Lámina sees how you look at him."

Mateo shrugged. "No. He doesn't share my interest. Regardless, I have no desire to be handed over to a stranger as a prize, expected to find affection where there is none."

"There's something you are not telling me."

Mateo ran a hand through his hair and looked away from Lámina's deep-set eyes. He thought of his father standing beside his mother's grave. He recalled the way his father's shoulders still shook with sobs whenever he remembered their joy and her death. "Truth be told, I don't wish to marry at all. Marriage for love only ends in grief. And marriage for any other reason is far too unpalatable."

"And what of lusts? Of urges?"

Mateo shrugged. "They can be satisfied without love or marriage, surely. I've heard as much admitted among the knights."

Lámina clucked her tongue. "Oh no, you don't cause trouble at all, *mi pájaro*. Blaming your sisters when you bring the greatest trouble of all."

Mateo looked up to the sky, squinting into the sun. "Is a full commitment of heart and soul really necessary for happiness, Lámina? Must I give my heart to another person when trusting in someone leaves me exposed to such pain that I could be wrecked for all eternity? I don't wish to end my life like father, sad and clinging too hard to his children."

Lámina's fuzzy brows lifted, white caterpillars smugly inching toward her hairline. "You will see for yourself, Mateo. Love is not something you avoid or throw to the dogs. Love is always the victor when it seeks you out. And you are marked by love."

Mateo sighed. He should have known better than to allow himself to go so far off course in this conversation. Lámina was a romantic old fool, overly fond of fairy stories and too full of love for him and his sisters to believe in anything but her own rose-colored dreams for them. But the problem was not his future and whether love would play a part, but rather if he would find himself forced into a marriage to King Hernandez, or some other equally unwanted chancer.

"Lámina, my sisters are the issue here. And yes, I suppose if I'm honest there is little to wonder about in their rebellion. Luz is of age now, and the others grow restless. They've all put our own lives aside for Papá's happiness. That cannot last forever."

"I dare say it has already come to an end."

"I know you have talked with father about his plans for the girls in the past." He reached down and rubbed a piece of sage between his fingertips.

"For you and for your sisters, yes."

Mateo's head snapped up. "What sorts of plans for me?"

"Only whether there are any princes in neighboring kingdoms who share your inclination toward other men." Lámina stared at the rosemary, her eyes distant as she considered.

"And are there?"

"Indeed, *mi pájaro*. There are a few. But your father never found one he favored for you. Nor any prospects that he deemed proper for your sisters."

Now it seemed his father had grown less particular in his choices for his children. Or perhaps it was only desperation and a loss of control over his wayward daughters that had left him willing to compromise them all without regard for affection, politics or bloodlines.

"If King Hernando has anything to do with it—" Mateo broke off, unwilling to contemplate that any further. It must not happen. He must find a way to discover his sisters' secret himself.

Lámina raised an eyebrow as she considered him, as if he'd spoken his thoughts aloud.

"I intend to put an end to this contest for our hands, Lámina. But I need help."

Lámina's old eyes were a strange gray-green that seemed to shift like the water of a deep lake. She studied him and he let her. For the entire length of an evening birdsong she studied him. "Come," she said.

Mateo realized he'd been holding his breath. He let it out slowly and followed where Lámina led, just as he had since he was able to walk. Lámina's cottage was small, messy and overflowing with dried herbs. No place in the kingdom smelled as pungent and aromatic. Mateo took a deep breath as he stepped inside.

"I have something for you," she said, motioning to him with her crooked, bird-claw fingers toward the dark shadows at the back of the cottage. "Something I've been waiting to give you for quite some time."

The cloak was of a dark but indeterminate color. It could have easily been blue, black or green in hue, but in the shadows Mateo could not say. The material was finer than anything Lámina could possibly afford, and Mateo opened his mouth to ask how she came by it. More importantly he meant to reassure her that he had no need for such a gift. He had many cloaks to his name, and would never want her to part with such a handsome object.

But Lámina stood on her tiptoes to press a finger against his lips. Mateo towered over her and not for the first time, he wondered at her smallness. Although he was as tall as the knights of the court, her arm was stretched to its full length just to keep her long nail pressed against his mouth, and only children were so tiny.

"Hush now," she whispered. She took

her finger away and lowered herself down to her flat feet. "You have always been my favorite. I want nothing more than to see you happy, loved, cherished, adored. You will need a young man who can match you pleasure for pleasure, thrust for thrust. I know you, my Mateo. I know what you seek."

Mateo felt the roots of his hair grow hot at the accuracy of her words.

"That's why you came to me. You know old Lámina will help you get it." Her eyes glinted in amusement. "Unless I am wrong? And you do seek to marry the old man with sour breath and a shriveled prick?"

Mateo could only laugh and shake his head.

"I thought not. This cloak is no ordinary cloak. It's woven with magic. Shh, don't ask how or why or where. I'll never tell. It is my secret and promise. The wearer of the cloak is invisible."

Mateo looked at the cloak in his hand.

He was skeptical but could think of no point in his life when, aside from fairy tales and stories, Lámina had ever told him or his sisters an untrue thing.

"Try it on. Walk about. See that no one will take notice of you so long as you wear it."

Mateo shook the cloak out and swung it around his shoulders. He felt unchanged, but when he turned to look in the mirror hanging on the opposite wall, he gasped. He was invisible as Lámina promised, from head to toes.

"How you use it is up to you," Lámina said, moving to her table, mounded with flowers in all stages of drying. She began to tie up the ends of the rosemary she'd brought in. "You could give it to King Hernando to aid him in his mission should your feelings toward him soften. Or, you could use it yourself to hide in your sisters' rooms, to watch how they rid themselves of old Hernando's unwanted presence and follow where they go."

Mateo took the cloak off. Yes, he was visible in the mirror again. He started to laugh, a giddy bubble bursting in his chest. "This is amazing, Lámina. Amazing!"

"It is," she agreed. "Oh, but I forgot one important thing."

"Yes?" Mateo asked, whipping the cloak over his shoulder again and watching his reflection wink out in the mirror.

"Old Lámina said you would be invisible, and that is true. Invisible to all but one."

Mateo slipped the coat off again, distracted. "All but one," he repeated slowly.

"Yes. The one who sees you despite the cloak's magic is…how shall I say?"

"Dangerous?" Mateo asked.

Lámina's eyes flickered as though she was holding something back. "Is special. ¿*Comprendes*?"

"*Sí. Un amigo.*"

"Not just any friend, Mateo. Your best friend."

Mateo frowned. "Luz is my best friend."

Being seen by Luz would defeat the purpose of the cloak, at least as far as his half-formed plan went.

"Not Luz," Old Lámina said, waving the idea away. "A different kind of friend than she could ever be."

"Then who?"

"Time will tell. Or perhaps time will not tell. In all the worlds seen and unseen, only one such person exists for you, Mateo. Do you get Old Lámina's meaning?"

Mateo held the cloak up, staring at its darkness, wondering what man might be the answer to the riddle the cloak contained. "I believe I do. The cloak not only renders me invisible, but reveals my truest friend."

"*Sí*, I believe you understand old Lámina now." She toddled over and patted his arm, gazing up at him with her deep, sea-like eyes.

Mateo's throat felt dry as he whispered, "Do you know his name?"

"Shh," Lámina's smile was as tender as when he was a child and he cried out in the night, terrified of the dark. "Let us make a bargain. You solve the problem of your sisters, and if you still don't know the name of your friend, Old Lámina will whisper it to you."

Mateo's heart pounded as he considered her words. "I accept, Lámina," he whispered. Then he stepped close, put his arms around her and kissed the top of her head. "*Gracias*."

LÁMINA HAD NOT been lying—of course she had not. Mateo wandered the castle, the grounds and the stables, and no one noticed him at all. It was the most freedom Mateo had ever experienced. The cloak's magic worked perfectly on people, but with animals not as well. The horses seemed oblivious to him, but, Whitey, his sisters' Bichon Frise, little fluffball that he was, barked and barked and barked in Mateo's general direction until Herminia and Elisa scolded the poor animal harshly and cast him out of their presence.

Mateo smirked as the dog trotted along beside him through the castle, yipping and nipping at his heels. The guards were befuddled, but they thankfully blocked the dog's way. In the dovecote, Mateo stood in the middle, waiting to see if the birds noticed him. He smiled softly when Pura swooped low, landed on his shoulder and cooed.

"All right," he said, pulling a loose thread from the end of the cloak and letting the dove take it from his fingers for her nest. Then Mateo pitched his voice to sound as authoritative as the men in his father's council who pounded their fists on the table as they demanded something or someone be shown the power behind the king.

"Tonight, I put an end to it. I will discover the truth of where they go once and for all."

The dove seemed impressed by his performance, and Mateo lifted his chin in half-amused pride.

Chapter Two

King Hernando pressed a gold ducat into the guard's palm. "Thank you for your good service. My men shall take over from here."

Mateo stood to the side, secure beneath the cloak and close enough that he would not miss his opportunity to follow King Hernando into his sisters' chambers. His father brandished the sole key to the door, which he now kept with him at all times. He even slept with it tied around his waist beneath his nightshirt. Such was his obsession with discovering the girls' secret, and so strong was his suspicion that an accomplice yet lurked in the court.

"I do wish Prince Mateo had joined us for dinner," Hernando said. "It would have been encouraging to see his face before this endeavor. I find his sweet brown eyes so fortifying, and his clean-shaven cheek a pleasure to touch."

Mateo shuddered, remembering the man's fingers on his face that morning at breakfast, claiming Mateo had a smear of jam on his cheek had been all the excuse necessary. The caress had been more than enough to solidify Mateo's resolve that the man's fingers never touch another inch of him again.

"My children's lack of manners and gratitude wounds me daily," his father said, looking grieved indeed. "Had they more of either we would not be in this situation. Their mother would be ashamed."

Mateo swallowed back his urge to dispute that. It was at times like this he had to admit to himself that, as the youngest, he and

Luz had not really known their mother. She existed for them only in stories. Perhaps his mother *would* be ashamed of them. Thinking of his sisters and their unbecoming defiance, perhaps she should be.

"I assume Mateo's dark, curly hair comes from your late queen," Hernando said, as if he'd not heard the tone of sadness in Mateo's father's voice.

"His hair, his mouth, all that is good of him."

The king unlocked the door and stepped inside the rooms. Mateo could hear him demanding the girls line up, and he called each of their names beginning with Adelita and ending with Luz, confirming they were all present.

Mateo plugged his ears as Hernando's men set up the giant bell, already dreading the noise of it. Silent, silent, do not breathe, do not make a sound, he reminded himself as he took position behind Hernando.

When Hernando was called upon to

enter, Mateo slipped through the door with him and into the darkest corner of the antechamber. He adjusted the dark cloak over his shoulders and watched as his father swept past with Whitey growling softly in his arms. Mateo was sickened to see his father's face so sad and drawn. Yes, it was time to put an end to his sisters' escapades. Even if Mateo himself chafed at his father's control, he wouldn't see him so heartbroken.

As the lock turned in the tumbler, Mateo stepped into the light from the large candelabras on the walls. He waited. Then he waited longer. Finally, the bell clanged, rattling him to the core, and he used the distraction of the noise to edge open the inner door leading to his sisters' bed chamber. In the open doorway he paused, half-expecting that the cloak's magic would not work, despite having tested it all day.

Through the door from the inner ante-room, he could see his sisters in their bedchamber, all wearing thick nightgowns and braided hair. They rested in their beds, facing King Hernando, who sat across from them in a straight-back chair at the writing desk. Most of them paid the king no attention as he prattled on about his own genius and his plan for the bell.

After several minutes, the bell rang again, drowning out his words, and Herminia frowned and stabbed a needle back and forth through fabric, drawing more blood than thread with each jab. Gracia and Josefina both read books, and several of the others talked quietly.

Mateo sank down to the floor of the antechamber as quietly as he could, his legs already growing tired of the aimless standing. When the bell stopped reverberating through the rooms, Hernando had moved on to the various changes he planned to make to his largest estate in order for Mateo to be more comfortable there.

"I believe the boy likes doves, does he not?"

"He does," Luz agreed, and Adelita shot her a dark look. "What, now? Are we to lie to him about what our brother likes?"

Adelita just glared at her and grabbed a brush from her vanity, starting to work out a knot in her hair.

"I intend to build a magnificent dovecote for him, bigger and better than any he's ever seen," King Hernando said. "It renders me nearly delirious to think of how he might smile when he sees it. Think how many doves he can raise! Do you think that would please him?"

"Do you think that will make him any happier to taste your prick?"

Mateo barely stifled his gasp, horrified by Imelda's comment. He waited for his sisters' reprimands to fly, but none did. They instead stared at King Hernando as if they wanted his answer. The man turned bright-red and gulped his wine down, coughing.

Catalina climbed from her bed, a contrite expression on her face, and poured the

King another draught. "There," she said softly. "That should help."

"Doves…" King Hernando started again, sounding a bit dreamy suddenly, as if he'd spent hours in his cups. "They are delightful, honest things. And so smart. Like your brother. He is no doubt as pure as a dove."

"No doubt," Imelda supplied. "For no man has dared try his ass. Is that what you dream of, King Hernando? Our brother's sweet, round ass?"

King Hernando looked scandalized. "Is this how you do it, then," he pondered, his words slurring as he took another long swig of wine. "Do you show yourselves so crass that…that…" He blinked, looking somehow stupider than he had only moments before. "Oh." He concluded, and then doubled over, passed out in the chair.

"Good Lord, he is a monster," Imelda said, tossing aside her sheets and stretching high. "We are saving our brother a great deal with this one."

"A monster?" Josefina asked. "For wishing to build Mateo something wonderful to make things easier for him? I rather thought he was kinder than I expected. Though not the right man for Mateo, naturally."

Each of his sisters climbed out of bed and pulled on fresh pairs of pale-pink slippers, delivered that evening to the castle from the shoemaker in the town.

"Luz," Adelita instructed. "Go check the antechamber. Ensure no one else lingers inside."

Mateo scrambled back, sitting very still under the portrait of their mother hanging to the right of the bedchamber door, and bit the inside of his cheek. The bell rang yet again, making him feel quite secure that none had heard his clumsy movement.

Luz carefully tried the main door. Then, sniffing at the air, she froze in place. She turned around slowly, scanning her eyes over the dark corners of the antechamber. Mateo's heart hammered as her eyes fell on him, but then skimmed away.

"Mateo?" Luz shoved a long, curly strand of black hair off her forehead, revealing her shining brow. Her frown was accompanied by her usual sharp commentary as she moved aside the curtains and tapestries on the opposite wall. "Too much cologne, Mateo. Sir Franco won't be seduced merely from the scent of cloves and musk wafting across the court. I am certain you must actually speak to him to make your intentions known, little brother."

Little brother. As if nine minutes made such a difference. Mateo held perfectly still, hoping that Luz wouldn't walk into him in her search.

"Mateo?" she sounded confused, but then straightened her back. "My imagination is playing tricks on me." Luz returned to the bedchamber.

Mateo waited a moment before creeping on his hands and knees back into the doorway to watch. His sisters were now in various states of dress and undress. Luz was the only one who made no move to change from her nightgown. The others had put on fancy dresses or were in the process of donning one.

Mateo generally didn't pay attention to his sisters' attire, but he could tell by the material that they were all quite fine, the frills and shine of them fit for a ball. He wondered if he were to throw off his cloak and barge in now whether they would all claim that they were only dressing for bed. He could imagine the tale Delfina would spin about why she was preparing to sleep in a diamond necklace and drop-pearl earrings.

"There was no one?" Gracia asked Luz. She tightened Adelita's corset a bit before helping her step into a dress of blue-and-white sky.

"Mateo?" Luz said uncertainly.

The sisters' heads all snapped up and searched the doorway where Mateo stood. Seeing no one, they went back to their powders and ribbons and perfumes.

"Is he gone?" Felipa asked.

"Yes." Though Luz didn't sound convinced. "I'm not sure he was ever there at all. I only caught the scent of him."

"Ah, yes. Mateo's cologne." Gracia laughed softly. "Who does he imagine it will impress?"

"Maybe Mateo has softened toward him," Herminia said, nodding toward the drugged and snoring king. "Perhaps our baby brother came to wish his future husband luck." Her hands sifted through the jewelry box on the desk in front of her and finally came up with a sparkling comb encrusted with diamonds. She shoved it into the bun at the nape of her neck, and preened in the mirror.

Mateo barely held back a small gasp. Herminia had never shown interest in jewelry before. She preferred men's clothes and had convinced the caballeros to teach her to spar. Even when attending court functions or balls, she preferred to wear plain, functional gowns and never applied paint to her lips or cheeks.

"I'm glad old King Hernando drank the wine so quickly. I could not bear it if he'd begun to tell us his dreams of poor Mateo's wedding night," Josefina said as she twisted her hair up in a complicated manner.

Luz looked over her shoulder toward the open door, and Mateo felt her gaze burn into his chest. For a moment he wondered if she could see him after all.

"Mateo," Elisa snorted. "He is in the palm of Papá's hand."

"He cannot be trusted," Adelita added, applying a dab of pink paint to her mouth.

"Don't say that," Luz said sharply, and Mateo noted how all the sisters looked her way before busying themselves again, focusing anywhere but on Luz. "Mateo is better than you credit him."

"Oh come, Luz!" Gracia interjected. "You know as well as I do that his temper would override all else. He would consider it his duty to defend our honor."

"Indeed," Adelita said. "He might not be as protective as Papá, but he's still too gallant for his own good, especially when it comes to proving himself entirely grown. And wouldn't this just be his chance?"

Luz frowned. "But given his leanings, it seems possible that he really might be the one."

"In time," Adelita said, cutting her off. "The joy of so many can't be put at risk in order to test a theory. We will continue as we have until we know for certain."

"But what of Mateo's joy?" Luz crossed her arms over her chest in defiance. "Doesn't he deserve to be as happy as the rest of us?"

Adelita threw up her hands. "Darling, we don't even know if he's the one."

"He must be. It is quite obvious."

Adelita groaned. "They are all expecting another sister. Admittedly, it's been since he was a babe in arms, but last I saw the parts in question he was decidedly not a sister."

"Yes, the last waits for a bride," Elisa chimed in.

"But!"

"Mateo can't be trusted, Luz," Gracia said. "He'll report us to Papá as surely as the sun rises and sets."

"There now," Blanca said, rising from her ornate vanity to put her arm around Luz's shoulders. "Let's not argue." She glanced at Gracia and Adelita. "Or pick on our little brother, whom we all adore. Are you not going with us, Luz? You know you must attend!"

"There's no question about that. Of course I'm going."

"Why are you not dressed?"

"It doesn't matter what I wear," Luz said softly, red creeping up her neck.

A frisson passed between the sisters, each of them seeming to burn a little brighter.

"No, I suppose it does not," Blanca agreed. She pressed her hand against her bosom and her eyes gleamed with something akin to fever.

"Mateo really does wear too much cologne," Elisa said, her nose wrinkling. "Someone should tell him. I'm quite sure Princess Sara will not find it at all nice to hold a handkerchief to her face so that she may breathe while she courts him."

"Perhaps he wears it to ward off the princesses," Adelita said.

"Princess Sara is to be the next to try, then?" Felipa asked. "It's unfortunate that she won't succeed. And while Mateo would not enjoy her as a wife, I've always liked her rather well. She's a delightful correspondent."

"Prince Leon has been added to the list," Gracia broke in. "I think he's a good match for Mateo. Handsome, funny and properly inclined from what his older sister writes."

"If King Hernando is too old, Prince Leon is too young. Just a boy. He hasn't even grown a beard." Adelita waved off the idea.

"Do you think there is no hope that Mateo may find something appealing in

Sara?" Herminia asked, a gentle note to her voice. "She's a good huntress. She brought down three deer on the last visit she made. Do you remember?"

A collective groan went through the room. Mateo wondered how long his sisters had been so interested in his marriage prospects. He'd not even known they cared.

"Please, spare us waxing on about the lovely Sara," Adelita said. "As for Mateo, we all know he longs for stronger things than any princess can give him." She held up her hand to stop Herminia from speaking. "Three slain deer from a feminine hand will not suffice."

"Unless she hides more than a shocking skill with the bow behind those muddy riding skirts, he'll never be interested in her," Imelda added, her black eyes snapping in amusement.

Herminia didn't reply, her face going dreamy.

"Ah, look at her. She thinks of the green

fields beneath Cacatúa's skirts," Imelda said with only a touch of a sneer.

Cacatúa?

Herminia grabbed a folded fan and threw it at Imelda. "Shall I tease you about the way you nearly toss up your own skirts at the sight of Gallo?"

Toss her skirts up? For a rooster? Mateo's heart raced. Was he hearing all of this correctly? Had Imelda been compromised, and willingly? And Herminia too, with a woman called, of all oddities, Cacatúa? Such names befit travelling performers, not courtiers, and where would his sisters meet such folk?

Mateo stared at each of his eleven sisters, trying to see if any stain appeared on their faces or bodies that would tell him if they'd been ruined already. The bell rang again, an aching sound that shook the furniture in the room. King Hernando slumped so that his hands touched the rug.

Then, as the irritating reverberation from

the bell passed, his sisters' clock struck the hour. The comparatively gentle sound swelled in the room and seemed to stretch into a pulse that beat with anticipation. Everything slowed, the air itself moving in visible currents. Mateo's heart pounded in his chest, his throat and mouth dry while his sisters transformed in front of him. They grew brighter, as if someone had lit hundreds of candles behind their eyes. Each of them became nearly too beautiful to look at, and Mateo lifted a hand to shield his eyes from their light.

"The window," Luz said, her skin glowing as though she was made of shifting sunlight. "It's time."

The casement grew and flexed, and to Mateo's amazement, the glass seemed to crinkle and then vanish as a set of three steps appeared before it. Adelita guided Catalina first, and the other sisters lined up behind her, with Luz taking the rear. To his disbelief, Catalina and Adelita walked up the stairs together and stepped out the window holding hands. Miraculously, they did not fall to the cobblestones below, but instead appeared to briefly walk on air before they disappeared.

Mateo stuffed his fist into his mouth to keep from crying out. Luz turned back, her eyes searching the space around where he was standing. Shaking her head, she faced her sisters. "Hurry, the window will close soon. We don't want to miss it."

"You are quite eager, Luz," Imelda said. "Wearing only a shift to make it easier for him. Urging us to make haste. What would Father think? Or Mateo?"

"As if propriety matters now," Luz shot back, stepping behind Imelda up the three stairs. "Just hurry, will you?"

Mateo rushed up behind Luz. At the top of the stairs he hesitated, his stomach in his throat, staring at the stones below. They were near the top of the castle, far above the trees in the courtyard. He watched his sisters walking on air. Luz waited until all the others had disappeared before stepping out herself.

It took all the trust in Mateo's soul to step out of the window. When he did, he found he did not fall, and the air was as solid as earth beneath him. The stars grew so bright that he could not see. The wind rushed around him and he shielded his face with his hand.

For a moment Mateo was overwhelmed with the urge to retreat to the safety of the castle. Then he strode onward, into the abyss.

<h1 style="text-align:center">Chapter Three</h1>

THEY WERE IN a wood—but no ordinary wood. The trees were tall and shaped like maples and oaks, but were heavy with silver leaves. Mateo reached out to touch, and the metal felt cool and bright, like pure moonlight against his fingers. He tugged on the shining leaf until it broke free. He quickly stashed it in his pocket as his sisters turned at the snap.

"Did you hear that?" Catalina asked.

"It was a deer," Adelita said. "Come, we're all here now and we mustn't keep them waiting."

The ten eldest started off into the woods

in their usual way. Adelita, Blanca and Catalina in the lead as the others followed arm-in-arm with their birth-mates, whispering in excited tones. Luz alone lingered, searching the forest behind her and sniffing at the air. Finally Luz gave up and followed her sisters. Mateo kept her in his sights.

The way was not short. As they walked, the silver forest gradually gave way to another wood of burnished gold. The golden glow cast from these leaves lighted his sisters' dark hair with fire, and drew out the warmth of sun from their skin so that they more resembled fantastical paintings on the castle's gallery wall.

Mateo didn't dare risk breaking another leaf from a branch, but many lay scattered on the ground glinting in the moonlight. He quickly bent to pick one up, putting it into his pocket next to the silver leaf he'd taken earlier.

The golden forest shifted into diamond-laden trees, and Mateo blinked in the dazzle.

The light from the moon glittered wildly against hundreds of facets in every leaf, blinding in its opulence and beauty. Mateo didn't resist. He reached out and tore one of the leaves from the tree. Luz glanced behind her at the noise, but the other sisters were oblivious, moving ever more swiftly, their skin dancing with rainbows of refracted light.

They no longer looked human, but like multicolored birds who might take flight. Mateo glanced down at his own skin beneath the cloak and saw that he too appeared as a changeling. It was a delirious illusion brought on by the unearthly light from the trees—his sisters were still women, and he still a man.

Just when Mateo began to doubt they would ever stop walking, the diamond forest opened onto a dark, wide lake. It was bigger than any lake he'd ever seen, with no end on the horizon. The moon on the waves left the impression of a glowing, heaving bosom, or the rolling flesh of man mid-coitus. Mateo felt stirring in his groin as he watched the waves move in relentless rhythm.

There had been no male in the court he could trust to bed, not even once he came of age. Despite the courtiers vying for his favor, offering with simpering smiles to bend over for him if only to gain power, not a one of them had been daring enough to give him what he'd needed. But the dark, undulating lake brought to mind all the lust-fueled dreams that had long left him in a sweat, shaking with desire.

He tore his gaze away from its seductive depths—and found in the water before them a row of strange men standing tall in wide, flat-bottomed boats that were half-filled with flowers.

Adelita approached the first boat. The man who helped her in was of the most extraordinary appearance. His clothing was of an unusual style, colored in the most vibrant hues. In fact, Mateo realized, his garments appeared to be made entirely of feathers. And though Mateo could hardly believe it, the man's hair was the yellow of a sunflower, and just as that flower follows the sun, his eyes followed Adelita walking toward him. He took her hand, kissed it with a redder mouth than Mateo had ever seen and guided her to sit.

Blanca approached the second boat. The man who helped her inside had hair the colors of pink roses and sky twirled together. His nose was rather beakish, lending an avian air to his face. He brought Blanca's hand to his lips and helped her settle before passing a bright-pink rose to her, then starting out across the lake.

Like balloons floating barely above the ground, his sisters drifted to the boats and climbed in, exclaiming over the flowers. It was only when Herminia approached that Mateo realized not all of the men were…men. Herminia's boat was command-ed by a woman with dark hair twisted into the shape of a birdcage. The woman's dress was of white and black feathers, with blue-green trim. Herminia did not simply take her hand to climb in, but kissed it passionately.

Imelda was next and Mateo did not hold back his gasp as she allowed the man with red-and-purple hair to pull her into a close embrace, nearly tipping over in their enthusiasm. He could not believe his eyes when the man reached below to cup Imelda's sex, and she did not cry out or bat his hand away, but leaned into the touch. Mateo turned his eyes resolutely away as their lips met.

He was relieved when Luz merely allowed the man with clover-and-sky hair to kiss her fingers before she sat down opposite him, smoothing her nightgown. In the face of all the unbelievable things Mateo had experienced so far that night, his sister wearing her nightgown outside her chambers was certainly the least shocking, and yet he noted the impropriety with dawning comprehension as he watched his twin sail away.

One boat remained.

The man in this boat was as startling to look upon as the rest. He was smaller than the rest of the creatures, his hair short and quite pink, sticking up in all directions as though he'd just woken from sleep, or perhaps never used a comb. He wore a riot of colored feathers woven into a shirt and breeches made of the softest brown leather Mateo had ever seen. Mateo's own fine woolen trousers and exquisite silk-trimmed tunic seemed almost shabby in comparison to the wild wonder before him.

The man's lips were the same pink as his hair, and his eyes were blue, fierce—as though they contained a soul stronger than his form. Mateo's blood coursed. He was as captured by the look of this man as he'd been captivated by the sensual lure of the water. Mateo swallowed hard, hesitating. Did he dare get in? He must to follow his sisters.

Mateo stepped forward and the creature smiled. Frozen in place, Mateo checked that he still wore the cloak. Lámina's voice echoed in his mind. The one who sees you despite the cloak's magic is a friend.

"Ópalo!" the man rowing Luz called as distance grew between his boat and the shore. "Next time, perhaps."

Ópalo, for that must be his name, did not look away, keeping his eyes on Mateo's own. "One moment more." He quirked his lips into a small, amused smile and rested his oar against the side of the boat.

Mateo took a step forward and Ópalo's eyes lit up. He lifted his chin slightly, almost imperceptibly, with a motion that indicated Mateo should come. Mateo lifted his hand in a small wave, and Ópalo nodded his head and smiled. It was a toothy, pretty thing that made Mateo catch his breath and take a step back.

Surely not.

"Come!" Luz's man called again.

"Patience, Azulejo!" Ópalo answered.

"We must not be late to the dancing."

"You must not. I can be as late as I wish."

"Stay then, and yearn for your bride to come. It changes nothing," Azulejo said before bending himself to the oars, speeding Luz away at an alarming rate.

Seeing Luz's white nightgown and dark, shining head disappear across the lake broke Mateo from his shocked state, and he quickly clambered into the boat with Ópalo. He ignored the offered hand as he stepped aboard, causing the boat to rock dangerously, nearly toppling them both out. Mateo's stomach lurched, and there was a spray of cold water against his face as Ópalo steadied the boat with his oar, digging it into the bottom of the lake. Mateo sat down quickly.

"Pardon me!"

Ópalo grinned, his blue eyes—blue as a summer sky—twinkling, and his lips spread again into that beautiful smile. "No need to be so formal."

Mateo wasn't sure what to make of the

casual tone, but there was nothing customary about the situation. He'd traveled with his sisters into a magical realm while hidden beneath a cloak that rendered him invisible, and which had apparently determined in some unfathomable way that this man, of all men, was to be Mateo's friend. He knew he should find more comfort in that, but he felt quite the opposite. It was hard to concentrate over the ceaseless thrumming in his veins.

Ópalo went on. "I'm so glad you came. I've waited for you. You have no idea how long."

Up close, Mateo could see that Ópalo seemed made of the shifting light from the diamond forest, his skin a mottle of beautiful colors that glowed breathtakingly in the moonlight. His eyebrows and eyelashes were pink, like the hair on his head, except that none of it was hair. Instead he had feathers, longer and thicker on his head, but short and fine around his eyes. His eyelashes appeared to be the daintiest feathers that Mateo had ever seen. And Mateo, out of either the arrogance of royalty or the shock of the moment, reached out a hand to feel them, only pulling back from touching the beautiful oddness at the last moment.

"I apologize."

Ópalo shook his head, and then reached out to grab Mateo's hand with a strong grip. He leaned forward, offering his eyebrows and hair up to Mateo's touch.

Mateo pulled back without making contact, a belated terror pumping through him. "Who? What?"

"Shh," Ópalo said softly. "They can hear. Sound carries over the water. You're hiding for a reason?"

Mateo swallowed, nodded his head, and realized he was shaking.

"There will be time to talk at the dance. Everyone will be busy and it's quite loud. Lean back. Relax. We'll go now." Ópalo's voice was warm and sweet.

Mateo sat straight as an arrow until the

rhythm of the waves and Ópalo's quiet regard lulled him. The water lapped against the side of the boat, the oars splishing and splashing as the boat glided smoothly on and on. The moonlight rippled against the undulating lake as far as Mateo could see. Perhaps it was not a lake at all, but an endless sea.

His limbs loosened, and Mateo discovered he was very tired. It was late, and he'd walked quite far. He leaned his head back against a cushion and looked at the night sky, seeing no constellation with which he was familiar. He brought his gaze back to Ópalo, who still studied him with intent admiration.

"Why do you watch me?" Mateo asked quietly.

"Haven't you ever been hungry?"

"Yes. Of course."

"When you're hungry and food is set before you, what do you do?"

The thrumming that had at last dissipated under the steady pull of the boat over the water roared through Mateo again. Could the cloak be wrong? Perhaps these people consumed humans and Ópalo was not a friend at all. Perhaps they were taking him and his sisters to be a feast for trolls in fairyland. For that's where they were, Mateo had no doubt. His sisters were in fairy thrall and now so was he, drowsing on a fairy lake, under the gaze of a fairy man with luscious lips and sparkling sky-colored eyes.

"Are you going to eat us?"

Ópalo's laughter was a joyous, riotous twitter of early morning birds in spring, and Mateo heard it echo across the lake. So much for being quiet. "Of course not, *mi pájaro*."

Mateo narrowed his eyes. My bird? Lámina sometimes called him that. It was quite the liberty, but no doubt things worked differently here, and Lámina had said that this man was meant to be his friend. Mateo cocked his head, took in Ópalo's handsome face, long neck and strong hands on the oars. Yes, perhaps somehow…more than a friend.

"Then what?"

Ópalo murmured, "I only mean that I can feast my eyes on you."

Mateo didn't say anything for a long time after that. There were too many questions crowding his mind. Finally, Mateo indicated his cloak. "How…?"

How did you know of the cloak? Why is it you who can see me when others cannot? How did you know I hid from my sisters? Who exactly are you and who are the others with my sisters? How, pray tell, has this come to pass?

Yet Mateo couldn't form the words.

"Lámina must have explained the cloak to you," Ópalo said.

Mateo sat up, jostling the boat. "You know Lámina?"

"She was once our old friend. She's the fairy who preferred to live with humans."

"Lámina?"

Ópalo chuckled softly. "Yes, that's her name." He went back to Mateo's previous question. "As for how—well, oh, surely you know?"

"We'll become friends."

Ópalo's cheeks flushed and the feathers on his head seemed to bristle. He rowed more quickly as he grew flustered. "Yes. Friends. So first, I hope you come to trust me."

Mateo's head churned faster than the oars dipping into the lake. "Trust you." He rubbed a hand over his eyes and peered around. "Truly this is all astounding. And Lámina is a fairy?"

"She was," Ópalo said. "When she left our world, she became something other. Closer to human, farther from fairy." As he said the words, the truth of them seemed so clear.

The details of the stories Lámina told them their whole childhood flooded Mateo's mind—a lake, fairies with feathers for hair, twelve lovers destined for twelve fae.

"FOR THE FAE lack your strength, children."

They were crowded onto and around Lámina's bed, all twelve of them. There was barely air to breathe, they all huddled so close. Even the eldest triplets had elbowed their way to good spots on the mattress next to Lámina's outstretched legs.

It was a special night, for Mateo and Luz no longer required the care of a nurse, and Lámina was to be given a cottage near a wide plot of land. There she could grow herbs and help Mateo with the dovecote being built for him. This was to be one of the last nights she would spend with the children in the castle.

Mateo felt tears burn his eyes at the thought of her leaving. But he was twelve, and it was nearly as embarrassing to have an old nurse tending to him as it was painful to let her go.

"Old Lámina tells you the truth! Fae cannot live as magical creatures in the human realm. Unlike you, who can pass back and forth with nary a change to your strong human blood. Every hour that a fairy spends in the human realm saps him of his essence, until eventually he may never return to fairyland."

"That's why they kidnap us," Imelda had said, her dark head rising above Mateo's own. "To marry us and have stronger children, ones who can pass between the worlds?"

Lámina shrugged and reached out to grip Mateo's chin, looking him over closely. "I suppose they'd take the lot of you as mates and happily spend their love on you, it's true. And your children could pass between the worlds more easily than those of fae blood alone. Though it's not just your children they want, but your human hearts as well. Listen to old Lámina. Human love strengthens and stabilizes their world. The royal family has always made alliances with humans, and always will.”

“Why? Is their world falling apart?” Mateo asked, imagining a world like the old dovecotes he’d seen while riding with his father, in need of strong beams to replace the old, cracking wood, and a coat of good plaster to hold the structure steady.

“It is at that,” Lámina said. “But aren’t they all, though?”

“Is it a structural problem?” Mateo went on. “Has a support beam gone bad?”

His sisters groaned and jostled about on the bed.

“*Sí*, it is just as you describe, Mateo.”

“Can’t they have a carpenter look at it?” he asked. “Love doesn’t seem like it would do much to fix a structural problem.”

“Worlds are not like dovecotes,” Lámina whispered, and all the sisters leaned close as they always did when she spoke quietly. No one wanted to miss a word, for Lámina’s secrets were always worth hearing. “Giving and accepting love is the real strength.

Remember that when the time comes. Remember that, *mi pájaro.*"

Mateo nodded up at her, mouthing the words "I promise" so that she smiled at him, showing her brown, stained teeth.

"And if the human doesn't love them?" Luz asked eagerly, if a bit bloodthirstily. "If the human heart isn't so easily theirs to enjoy? Will they perhaps eat it? A sort of heart-shaped cake?"

"Yes, Lámina," Imelda said, her dark eyes glinting. "Would they murder us with their sharp fairy claws and teeth?"

Lámina's smile was slow and kind, almost like she pitied Luz and Imelda for asking. "Listen to old Lámina. You love the fae. You always love them and they always love you. It is how it is. It is how it shall be."

Mateo felt the truth of her statement deep in his bones, and he settled in close to her, wanting to tell Lámina he loved her, but knowing his sisters would mock him for the babyish sentiment.

"Tell us the story of the fairy king and his twelve children," Adelita requested. "I haven't heard that one in years."

"Because you have been 'too grown up' for old Lámina's stories for years. Or so you've said as you scoff at your siblings for their bedtime tales." She scolded, but her voice was full of affection.

Adelita settled in closer, smiling at Lámina sweetly. Lámina reached for Luz and pulled her up to tuck under her other arm, freeing up a bit of space on the mattress for Gracia to slide into.

Beneath her warm chin, snug against her soft nightdress, Mateo's hand resting on her wrinkled, dry arm, Mateo vowed he would never be too grown up for Lámina's stories.

"In a kingdom very close and yet very far, there lives a fairy king and his twelve fairy children. Merry, smart and talented, they each await a chance at human companionship in hopes of strengthening their kingdom…"

Chapter Four

THE OARS HAD not ended their rhythmic splashing, and Ópalo still gazed at Mateo with the same steady expression as Mateo reeled in the memory.

"You've been expecting us."

Ópalo nodded.

"I apologize if I'm slow to understand, but I thought they were only stories."

"I find your confusion charming."

Mateo had no words for that, and instead latched on to a story from the memory. "Your father is the king of this realm?" Mateo confirmed.

"Was the king, yes. He died."

"*Lo lamento.*"

Ópalo smiled again, his eyes crinkling at the edges, his pink, feathered lashes brushing against his flushed cheeks. "You are very polite, *mi pájaro*. Truly, you are charming."

Mateo's stomach fluttered in response to the flattery.

"My eldest brother has inherited the throne of this land, and my siblings and I assist him as necessary." Here Ópalo motioned with his head to the other boats to illustrate his relationship to the fae escorting Mateo's sisters.

At least if his sisters had been compromised then it had been with royalty. Fairy royalty of course, but perhaps that was not so very terrible?

"When your sisters arrived without you day after day, I nearly despaired." Ópalo nodded to the east. "Look, morning breaks."

Mateo turned away from Ópalo and yes, the sun's rays broke over the horizon. The light cast the lake into a fiery sparkle, as though each wave was opal. His heart jolted and Mateo gasped. "It's morning! Papá! He'll see that we're gone!"

"Shh, quiet," Ópalo said, lifting one of his fine hands to silence Mateo. "Your father will still be sleeping. He'll sleep for days of our time. There's no need to rush. However, the portal is always open from our side. Whenever you wish to return simply say the word and I'll take you back to the shore."

"Always open on this side, but not on the other?"

"Your sisters tell us the portal only opens at night on your side, once a day for a short time."

"How short?"

"I don't know. It stays open for as long as it should, and not a moment longer. Magic doesn't often follow rules."

"But how? The portal leads to my sisters' chambers. This was by design?"

"I believe Lámina chose. I know little of her magic, except that it finally brought you to me. And that she made sure the portal was always open on this side, so you and your sisters can leave freely."

Mateo stared at the sunlight shifting on Ópalo's skin, washing away the rainbow opalescence of the night, and leaving him a pale, beautiful bird of a man. His feathers shone in the light, his eyes brighter than before, and his lips looked plump as pillows in the clear morning sun. There was no reason to believe him, and yet there was no reason to doubt him either.

Ópalo grinned. "You're very handsome. Dark as you are, with such red lips."

Mateo's face grew hot, his blood rushing pleasurably.

Ópalo didn't stop there. "And you're every bit more human than I could have hoped."

Everything about Ópalo was like gazing on something too good to be true, like the sweetest, most lovely cake the castle baker had ever constructed. Mateo felt sure that eating such a thing would leave him aching for more and less. It was tempting, but ultimately superficial. Mateo's pulse quickened, but he hardened himself. Friendship was one thing, but if this fairy intended to feast on love from Mateo's human heart, he was going to have to work harder than that.

"Nothing but sugar. Your words are too sweet and lack sustenance."

Ópalo's eyes laughed at him. "I see that friendship will not be granted without good cause, no matter what your cloak has declared."

"You see correctly. And you'll find I am not always so polite."

"You're quite forgiven. Look at the sunrise. Watch how it comes up over the bridge."

The bridge? Were they finally getting somewhere then?

Mateo turned and saw the boat carrying Luz slip beneath an arched stone bridge. On the other side was a castle—the largest, most ornate castle that Mateo had ever seen. As they rowed closer the light hit the great structure and Mateo gasped. Each cupola, each arch, every window and door casing—of which there were hundreds—and each buttress big and small were all built of birdhouses. White birdhouses, gold birdhouses, tangled together and stacked one upon another, a feat of design and engineering, lifting the castle into the blue sky.

As the shadow of the bridge passed over them, a trumpet sounded, and there was a great noise, the flutter of thousands of wings as a swirl of birds flew out of the houses of the castle and swept through the sky before careening back again, swooping low and screeching.

Mateo stared in wonder, shielding his head when some dropped exceedingly low and close.

"They won't hurt you," called Ópalo over the noise. "It's only our cousins welcoming your sisters home. And you, of course."

"Home?" Mateo turned to Ópalo. "How can this be their home when they've spent all their years in our father's realm?"

"Time is different here, *mi pájaro*."

The repetition of the odd endearment was a prickling reminder of how far out of his depth he was in this strange land. He felt dizzy and a little sweaty. The calling of the birds was too loud in his mind, and the amazing tower before him dwarfed all of his previous ideas of what was possible. "My bird? You dare to address a prince in this way? Not once but many times?"

"I do, yes."

"Do you care nothing for the possible consequences of such an affront?"

Ópalo's mouth twitched. "No. I do not."

Mateo narrowed his eyes. Being trapped as he was on a boat in the middle of the vast lake, he said only, "Such liberties! Speaking to me as a friend when you don't even know my name." Mateo drew up, attempting to look more regal, as he did when he practiced for court functions in the mirror. Ópalo seemed amused, which left Mateo rather certain he'd failed.

"Of course I know your name, Mateo. And you may call me Ópalo. Again, there's no need for formality here."

Confusion and curiosity warred within him. Mateo's eyes snapped to Ópalo's face.

"Luz speaks of you often." Ópalo volunteered in answer to Mateo's unspoken question. "She misses you terribly when she's here."

"You make it sound as if she doesn't see me every day."

"For Luz, many days pass between the few hours you spend together."

"*Time is not what it seems, children,*" Lámina said, her eyes hooded as if she was revealing a secret. "*In fairyland, a single night can last for days.*"

"When Lámina didn't send a bride

through for me, I was relieved at first."

A bride? Mateo stared. Of course, how had he not realized? Twelve lovers for twelve fae. He shook his head. What had Lámina done—and what had his sisters wrought?

Ópalo continued on as though unaware his words had set Mateo reeling. "Though I've lain with females and males, I always hoped to take a man as my love." Ópalo looked around, as though measuring who might be listening. Luz and her fairy man were quite a distance away, and it would be impossible to hear much of anything over the call of the swooping birds.

"When I listened to Luz speak of you, your kindness, your handsome face and the dedication you've shown to your doves, I couldn't help but hope that you might be *la hermana* intended for me."

Mateo's jaw flexed, his stomach flipping as images pierced his mind—debauched, delicious images of being this fairy's lover. Heat flooded through him, arousing—and terrifying. He gritted his teeth and clenched his fists. "I am no 'sister'."

Ópalo's mouth twitched and his eyes glittered with humor. "No, I can see you are not."

"I'm a prince."

"For which I am very glad."

"And when I return to give my father the news of my sisters' misadventures, I'll win the right to choose my own fate."

Mateo recalled the stories Lámina told and her certain voice. *"You love the fae. You always love them and they always love you. It is how it is. It is how it shall be."* As a child, he'd been certain too, never believing any of it could be real. But no more. This was no children's tale, and such love must be earned.

The power he sensed from Ópalo was enticing. Mateo couldn't deny the deep pull of it, and though on the surface the fairy seemed slight, there was something brutal and confident in his face. Mateo questioned his ability to resist Ópalo should it come down to it.

"My human heart is my own." Mateo put his chin up. Then a splat of bird shit landed on his sleeve.

Ópalo chuckled, reaching into a hidden pocket in his feathered shirt to bring out a handkerchief. "Favored already. I'm not surprised." He wiped at the dropping with the soft cloth and tossed it overboard. "A treat for the fish."

Reassured that Ópalo had not disputed his declaration as to the state of his heart, Mateo turned his attention to the doves as they swept by them again and again.

"Can they see me?"

"Indeed. All the cousins can. If anything will give you away before you're ready, it will be them. They mean no harm. They simply don't understand you're meant to be invisible."

A dove swooped low and cooed. Ópalo smiled in response and answered it.

"Yes. He's here for me." Ópalo gestured

at Mateo. "A youngest son for a youngest son."

Mateo opened his mouth to dispute this, but held his peace, because just as the birds had swept down suddenly upon them, they swirled away, some returning to their homes in the castle walls, others flying out over the lake.

"Earlier I spoke of hunger," Ópalo said. "Take my advice, *mi pájaro*. While you're here you may drink whatever you like, but you must eat nothing."

"Why?"

Ópalo seemed to dim slightly, and he looked away for the first time, gazing off to where the sun rose higher. The light played on his face. "So your human heart may remain your own for as long as you choose, unlike your sisters'." Ópalo's voice held a note of melancholy.

Mateo blanched at the idea that his sisters' hearts had already been given—and perhaps not of their choosing? "Are my sisters in danger?"

"Only if love is danger."

Mateo was about to demand a more thorough response when he saw that Adelita and Blanca's boats had arrived. They stepped onto a well-built wooden dock with their fairy men. Each of his sisters waited for her turn to disembark. As the boats crowded close together, Luz looked toward Ópalo with a curious, worried expression that lifted when Ópalo smiled at her.

"Ópalo!"

That was Adelita's voice. She stood by the edge of the dock and called to him. "I'm sorry you again waited in vain. We have no more sisters, as I've said before."

"I live in hope," Ópalo called to her.

Adelita seemed bemused by this optimism. "Hope will not create a sister where there is none!" She waved as her fairy man escorted her away.

"His name is Canario," Ópalo said softly for Mateo's benefit. "An eldest brother for an eldest sister, and so on down the line. And now there is you for me." Ópalo smiled.

"I am not a 'sister'," Mateo muttered again, wanting to make that very clear for some reason he couldn't put his finger on. He swallowed, confused as to why the words "and I am not for you" got stuck in his throat and refused to come out. Surely the cloak could not compel him to commit to something his heart did not feel?

"You are not a sister," Ópalo agreed. "But you should still take my hand when we disembark, lest you taste the cold of the lake."

Mateo swallowed his pride and did just that. When he released Ópalo's hand and stood before the great castle swarming with birds, having rowed miles across a lake so vast he'd never seen its like, Mateo stared in awe at the world around him. It was a jumble of beauty such as he'd never seen.

"Ópalo," he breathed, uncertain and amazed. The name tasted like sweetness on his tongue. "It's just as she said it would be, just like her stories described."

Ópalo's eyes softened. "Come. You're safe with me. I promise."

As they entered the castle, Mateo allowed Ópalo to retake his hand.

Chapter Five

Four Months Earlier…

TOES IN THE water, Ópalo sat by the edge of the lake, watching their bird cousins twist and dive in the air as his siblings decried their lot in life.

"The brides do not come." Canario moaned. "We wait and we wait, and yet they never come. Azulejo and Ópalo are of age now. What else could be holding Lámina back from sending them?"

"Perhaps the youngest bride hasn't joined them in adulthood?" Zafiro rubbed at his thick eyebrows so vigorously that the small feathers stood up from his face in red and orange ruffles.

Canario waved that off. "You know that's not possible. She's yet another twin, or so father said."

"She's the only reason Ópalo was even called into being," Tulipan said.

Ópalo never knew how he was supposed to feel about the fact that he'd been conceived solely to be the mate to a human child in order to complete his father's plan to strengthen their land.

"Yes, after the incident. And perhaps that is the problem. We wait because we have not yet had word from Lámina of the readiness of Ópalo's bride. All of us wanting and waiting, and for what? But he's not a true brother, only a half. Fate recognizes these things," Halcón said.

"I'm sitting right here," Ópalo noted, but his siblings ignored him.

"We should move forward without consideration for his…problem."

"I'm as much a member of this family as

the rest of you."

The others, especially his sister Cacatúa, rallied to him, agreeing wholeheartedly that he was not only their full brother in heart and spirit, but perhaps the best among them. "Your heart is full of love, and you are the most beautiful of us all," Cacatúa murmured in his ear as she caressed his feathers. "Halcón is only jealous. Ignore him, baby bird, just as you always do."

Ópalo didn't like the coddling any more than he liked the insult from Halcón, but he tolerated it. There was no escaping that he was youngest, and that they had all, except for Azulejo, cuddled, fed and dressed him when he'd been a tiny fairy. Given his mother had died in birthing him, his siblings had all cared for him more than most.

After everyone but Halcón had made some sort of amends to Ópalo for what had been said, Canario paced along the edge of the water. "Perhaps Halcón is right." He held up a hand to forestall Cacatúa's complaint.

"No, not about Ópalo. But maybe it's time to abandon waiting for Lámina's word and act for ourselves," Canario said, the leader as always.

Cacatúa clucked her tongue softly, sounding for all the world like her namesake, and she said, "But that's not proper, Canario. That is not the bargain that Lámina made with our father."

Since infancy they had been instructed to wait for Lámina to send the brides. When the brides passed through the threshold, the cousins would know, and they would alert the princes and princess to take the boats to the far side of the lake to await their lovers. Once in their presence, the brides, human as they were, would succumb to the siblings' natural fairy thrall. And once they'd consumed the food of fairyland, they would surrender to their natural passions. That was as it had always been, and as it would always be. Lámina's role was to make sure the brides came.

"Waiting has gotten us nowhere. Didn't Father also tell us that sometimes one must take matters into one's own hands?" Canario said with the particular flint in his tone that said the decision had been made and no amount of arguing would change his mind.

As Ópalo watched the cousins fly toward the portal that night, messages for the human brides tied to their feet, anxiety curled in his gut and he wished to call them back. He didn't want a bride. He never had and never would. He'd lain with many of fae blood, but did not wish to lie with a woman again, preferring to spend his pleasure on the men of the court. The idea of being tied to a human bride didn't please him at all. Perhaps a human woman would be somehow different, but Ópalo feared she would not. Deep inside, he wondered if his doubts had played any part in the delay of the brides' arrival.

Yet he didn't want to hold back his siblings any longer. They had all waited for such a long time. Ópalo had no idea what his brothers and sister had written to their prospective lovers, but his note was short and sweet.

Dear bride, come at once. Let us see what our future may bring.

ÓPALO HELD ONTO Mateo's fingers. He felt the strength in them, the pulsing warmth of blood bringing a heat to the surface of the skin. Fae were not so hot-fleshed as humans, though they were often just as hot-tempered—if not more so—and unfortunately lacking the scruples so many humans were rumored to hold dear.

As they followed the others into the castle, Ópalo kept an eye on Mateo's face, noting his expressions of awe and wonder, and the ripple of fear beneath it all. A protective affection rose within him, reminding him of his brothers' comforting arms around Mateo's sisters' shoulders the night they first arrived.

When Mateo had arrived at the edge of the lake—lush lips, golden skin, dark hair and brown, soft eyes wide with both fright and bravery—Ópalo had remembered his father once placing a precious red-skinned apple into his hand and saying, "This is from the human world."

Ópalo had kept it for days, delirious with its beauty and the potential of its crisp flesh. During that time, he'd learned much about the mysterious fruit. It promised to be delicious and meaty, yes, but it was also easily bruised. When he'd finally taken a bite, he'd nearly cried from the joy of it.

Mateo reminded him of that apple. Ópalo wanted to admire him for years, taking in every facet of his beauty, his textures and scents. He wanted to caress the tiny curls he could see just behind Mateo's ear, run his finger over the fringe of his eyelashes, and touch the small dimple in his chin. Then, only after an ecstasy of waiting, would he finally take a bite and consume him entirely—taking his love into Ópalo's body. Turning him into his strength. His heart.

As they'd rowed and talked, Ópalo had fallen in love. Yes, love. Because Ópalo was as ready for it as the night sky is ready for the stars to pierce it. Wide open and eager for light. It felt like flying, running, jumping, swimming and laughter all rolled into one vibrant emotion. Ópalo already adored Mateo's intoxicating mix of insecure arrogance and brave, kind heart.

And if Mateo wanted his heart to be his own, then Ópalo would keep it safe for him. Ópalo decided as soon as the words left Mateo's mouth that he would never use fairy magic to influence or secure Mateo's affections. Feeding Mateo a fairy cake would be easy enough. Ópalo had witnessed his siblings' successes in that regard, but there was little choice in that kind of love. If Mateo was to give Ópalo his heart, it would be of his own volition, even if it meant that Mateo, like the apple, might be damaged and bruised. Lost.

He imagined his siblings would find this foolish, but none of them had faced a human lover like Mateo. His sisters were all quite different from him—eager to be brides and to fall in love. Surely, though, he would not wait long for Mateo's affection. Patience would be rewarded soon, he was quite certain. How could Mateo resist the pull between them? He must surely feel it when Ópalo felt overwhelmed by it.

Ópalo squeezed Mateo's fingers as they stepped into the ballroom, the fairy glass tossing rainbows everywhere in pools of color, the tables laden with only the most beautiful spreads of cakes, meats and wines. "It's lovely, isn't it?"

"Yes." Mateo spoke quietly so his sisters wouldn't hear.

The musicians struck an opening chord,

bird cousins flew in to begin their symphony and the sisters were led to the tables. Each took up a cake in her fingers, and with varying expressions of eager expectation they took small, dainty bites. They accepted the wine Ópalo's brothers and sister offered and washed the rest of the cakes down.

"Are you hungry?" Ópalo asked.

"You told me not to eat."

"So I did, but that wasn't my question. Are you hungry?"

Mateo seemed to consider and then answered, "No."

Ópalo squeezed Mateo's hand. "This is important. You won't feel hunger, no matter how long you stay with us, but you will be tempted to eat anyway. Out of habit or curiosity for the food. Do not indulge, I beg of you."

"Why?"

While Mateo seemed impressed by the ballroom, the birds and the castle itself, Ópalo could see that his patience was wearing thin, and his nerves were fraying from the effort it took not to do something to gain control of his sisters.

"Fairy food, when consumed by humans, is a promise that can never be broken. They're bound to fairyland and their lovers forever, and must return to us at least once an earthly moon, or suffer greatly." Ópalo hesitated, but the rest needed to be shared as well. "There is an aphrodisiac effect as well."

He realized his error in revealing this information when Mateo began to unhook his cloak. Ópalo admired the flash in Mateo's eyes, the flush that rose to his face and his willingness to toss aside his own safety to save his sisters from that which they'd already succumbed to long ago. But things would only get very ugly if Mateo challenged Ópalo's siblings. He put a finger against Mateo's soft lips. "Shh, shh now, *mi pájaro*. It's too late. They've been here many times before and consumed much."

He held Mateo by the shoulders, feeling

the strength of his body. Eventually, the fight went out of Mateo with a long exhalation. Ópalo's chest constricted at the look of sad defeat on his face.

"Please don't take it so hard, Mateo," Ópalo said, grabbing a cup of wine from a passing servant. He pressed it into Mateo's hand. "Drink. This will calm you."

Mateo stared at the cup, but took a hesitant sip when Ópalo urged him again.

"*Mi pájaro*, they are consorts of my brothers and sister, the most respected fae in our realm. There is nothing to be upset about."

"Nothing? They are under a thrall. They didn't choose this."

"But they did. Your sisters knew the consequences of eating the cakes. They do so willingly, eagerly even. They longed for the freedom."

"Freedom?"

"From your father's control. From their own inhibitions. They came here with eyes open. I admit my siblings encouraged them, but your sisters' wildest dreams have come true. They are so very happy."

Mateo nodded, but looked a bit numb as he took several deep swallows of wine before speaking. "Are they here to stay then? Are we all here to stay?"

Ópalo wished he didn't sound unhappy with the thought. Was the idea of being here so very terrible? "They can come and go as they please, but they'll always return. That's the promise they made when they ate our food. The promise they gave joyfully." Ópalo smiled reassuringly. "Look, the dancing has started."

Ópalo wished he could view the scene through Mateo's eyes. He'd only heard stories of the human realm, first from his father, and later from Mateo's sisters, but he knew enough to understand that Mateo had never seen anything like what he was witnessing now.

The ballroom was large, the biggest space

in the castle by far, and made entirely of fairy-glass and platinum bars to hold the panes. The sun shone down into the room, setting the colors alight with a life of their own, pooling against the tile floor in some places, spinning and whirling in others. The birds and fae alike had thrown themselves into the dance—twisting, swinging, lifting and twirling, whether in midair or on the dance floor. They used their heels to drum the rhythm of the songs, whooping in delight as the festive mood escalated.

Luz and Adelita swirled by on the arms of Azulejo and Canario. The blue and white of Adelita's dress along with the yellow of Canario's feather hair combined reminded Ópalo of a summer day. Luz's billowing nightgown, mixed with Azulejo's blueness, was a cloud dancing with the sky. Glancing at Mateo, Ópalo saw that his eyes glittered with amazement. Pride in his world and the wild beauty it offered burst through Ópalo.

The feathers of birds and fae molted with

each climax of song, confetti of floating color echoing the vibrant cacophony of music, birdsong, delighted cries of fae and the human laughter of Mateo's sisters. A river of sound poured over them, smoothing away all roughness.

Soon, the atmosphere of the room became a wild torrent of joy, and Ópalo sensed Mateo softening to it, becoming caught up in the jubilant chaos. As he drank the wine, his expression lost the harsh edge of worry and took on the exaltation of awe. Mateo's eyes at first followed his sisters, but eventually left them to their fervent fairy-magic dancing as he began to watch the birds and the fae, gasping occasionally at some spectacular display. It wasn't long before Ópalo saw Mateo had relaxed. His head moved to the music and his limbs, which he'd held tightly since he'd roused from his relaxation in the boat, went loose and easy, swinging along to the beat. Ópalo's heart lifted in his chest, taking flight with emotion. If only Mateo would relax enough to understand their destiny together!

Cacatúa swung by in the strong arms of Herminia, faces flushed, eyes glowing and their lips wet and open from the kisses they'd already shared. Next Josefina and Narciso twirled past, oblivious to everything but the desire pulsing between them, and then Gracia spun by Zafiro's side, teasing him with her eyes, drawing him closer and pressing wantonly against him. Mateo's sisters were lost deeply in fairy magic, their bodies and mind spinning with lust and passion. Ópalo could see his own siblings were focused entirely on their conquests, eager to bed them, but dragging the torment of the sensual dancing on just for fun.

"They won't notice if we join in," Ópalo said, eager to feel Mateo's body against his own. He took Mateo's empty second cup from him and handed it off to a servant. "All the fae and your sisters are so lost in the revelry now, delirium has set in. Nothing we do will seem amiss."

Mateo's breath visibly quickened, and he kept his eyes focused on the crowded dance floor. He didn't answer, but licked his lips as his pupils dilated, tugging the cloak closer around his shoulders. Ópalo stared at his beautiful brown eyes, drawn into their bright warmth. He noticed the dark hair curled around the edge of the pink shell of Mateo's ears, and his chest ached with a need to possess Mateo as his own.

Shaking himself free of the spell of Mateo's beauty, Ópalo turned to Mateo and bowed. He offered his hand and said formally, "May I have this dance, good prince?"

A shock of lust and rightness set Ópalo's mind aflame as he placed his hand firmly in the small of Mateo's back and guided him into the steps. He looked up, meeting Mateo's eyes, which had taken on the same glow as his sisters' after they consumed fairy cakes. Delirium seemed to consume him as well, brought on perhaps by exhaustion, two cups of wine, too many new wonders and more than a little shock. Mateo soon moved against Ópalo without any measure of shyness, his arousal evident.

It was as Ópalo had told his siblings, though they hadn't listened to him. The thrall of fairy cakes wasn't necessary. A fairy's nature—sensual, sexual, free—would inspire lust, and the usual desired outcome would arrive easily enough. There was no need for aphrodisiacs, and once they'd brought each other pleasure, Mateo would love him soon, surely.

"I want you," Mateo whispered, amazement in his tone and his eyes dark with desire. "I've felt this before for men, but this is stronger. Tell me, is this how I'm meant to feel?"

"Yes." Ópalo pressed his cock against him, gratified when Mateo shifted his thigh into Ópalo's hardness.

"Is this what my sisters feel?"

"They feel it more. The cakes escalate their passion until it's unbearable not to act on their urges. Your sisters tell me that the immensity of sensation while under their influence is quite glorious."

Mateo bent low, his face dropping close to Ópalo's, his eyes focused on Ópalo's mouth. He whispered, "I'm envious then. Although I can't imagine feeling more than this."

The tempo picked up, and Ópalo led Mateo into the dance with focus and fervor, moving against him so that their arousal was unflagging. He directed Mateo easily, finding him shockingly pliant in his arms, eager to follow and be led. Ópalo burned with the images that came to his mind—Mateo in Ópalo's nest, Mateo yielding and eager, Mateo following Ópalo over the edge into a trembling climax. His heart overflowed with love at these thoughts. Ópalo drove them both harder, moving them across the floor, not caring if they bumped into other fae in their exertions. All in the room were lost in the dance. No one paid attention to jostling from an invisible dancer and his fairy.

Mateo was out of breath and a thin trickle of sweat ran down his stubbled cheek. Ópalo dragged Mateo's head down as he lunged forward, rubbing his own fairy-smooth skin against the grain of hair. It scratched enticingly and he shuddered, repeating the gesture. He wanted nothing more than to feel the scrape of Mateo's odd, human hair against his skin again and again. He wondered if he tasted as delicious and different as he felt?

Mateo groaned, and Ópalo was surprised by the tentative hand in his feathers, pulling his head closer with a delicious tug. His brows and scalp ruffled in anticipation.

"Perhaps a cake would serve me in good stead," Mateo said, his voice pitched lower than before, urgent.

"I don't believe you require one."

Mateo appeared feverish, and Ópalo's

gut clenched in rough desire. Mateo practically growled as Ópalo gripped Mateo's chin. When he didn't jerk away, Ópalo dove up for a kiss. The softness of Mateo's lips and the wet warmth of his tongue tasted even better than the apple of Ópalo's youth. Human and fairy saliva mixed in the eager crush of their mouths, tasting bright and sweet at once. The heat between them grew in urgency. He shoved against Mateo, pushing him out of the whirling dance and across the ballroom until Mateo's back hit the wall.

Dancing fae swirled past them, birds swooped and called, and on either side, down the stretch of the wall, couples moved together, kissing, arching, thrusting, skirts and pants shifted aside. Grunts, moans and cries added to the rush of sound in the room.

Mateo's eyes went dark and hot, his hips moving against Ópalo's with what seemed to be mindless desperation. "Where do we go, how do you take me?"

The promise of those words!

"Here," Ópalo said, his heart slamming happily against his chest. Lust swelled, his feathers bristling on his head, his cock throbbing. Kissing Mateo again, he pressed against him, trying to get more pressure. Mateo grabbed him closer, lifting him up to his tiptoes to kiss at a better angle and thrust his hips against Ópalo's own.

Ópalo pushed against his strong chest, struggling free of his arms.

"I'm sorry," Mateo started breathlessly, but Ópalo stopped his apology short by shoving his hand into Mateo's trousers to grip his hard, thick cock.

Mateo's mouth dropped open, round, soft and glistening red. Ópalo couldn't resist sucking on those lips as he moved his hand in rapid strokes. Mateo whimpered, gripping Ópalo's hips to drag him close, clutching at Ópalo's ass as he submitted to his kiss and hand.

Mateo's prick was hot, blood rushing

under the skin, heady, intoxicating and powerful. Ópalo stared into Mateo's wild eyes as he sucked Mateo's lips, licked the inside of his limp mouth and jerked his hand up and down the shaft of Mateo's cock, the sound of the dancers' heels pounding on the tiles behind them keeping the time. His heart danced with them.

Mateo moaned and shifted his feet. He released Ópalo's ass and clutched his feathers, gripping until the quills strained against Ópalo's scalp. Mateo's kiss became urgent, his lips moving roughly against Ópalo's, his tongue pressing into Ópalo's mouth. The sounds of Mateo's cresting passion swelled in the space around them and stirred every cell of Ópalo's being to thrilling joy.

Ópalo felt the surge, knew the moment was upon them, and with nimble, fast fingers, used his free hand to fully undo Mateo's trousers. He pulled out of Mateo's embrace, hearing the disappointed cry of denied release even as he felt the hard tile under his knees. He yanked Mateo's trousers down around his hips, freeing his cock and sac, taking a moment to admire the thick strength of Mateo's prick. He looked up to Mateo's face, struck by joyous lust at the sight of his dazed expression and wet lips.

Ópalo opened his mouth and in a quick move—perfected on many fae since he'd come of age—engulfed Mateo's cock, sucking him into his mouth before opening his throat to take him deeper. It throbbed against Ópalo's tongue with the rhythm of Mateo's human heart. Affection rose urgently through him and he stared up at Mateo, hoping Mateo felt the same connection.

"¡Dios mío!" Mateo moaned. His hands moved to Ópalo's feathers, gripping them hard enough for tears to sting Ópalo's eyes, but Mateo didn't move, simply gasping and staring down at Ópalo with a wild expression. Ópalo pulled off, licked the head and dove down again.

Mateo released Ópalo's feathers and

pounded his fists back against the wall, shaking helplessly as his climax hit. Spurt after spurt of salty human seed filled Ópalo's mouth and he swallowed it eagerly. He coaxed more from Mateo's shuddering flesh by sucking hard on the head of his prick, working the shaft roughly with his hand until Mateo squirmed and pulled desperately at Ópalo's feathers.

Ópalo stood, his own cock aching, but he helped Mateo straighten his clothes before buttressing his shoulder under Mateo's arm. Mateo slumped, panting, red-faced and beautifully human against the wall. It was intoxicating to see.

The dance went on behind them as Mateo shook and shuddered, limp in Ópalo's arms. Ópalo gripped Mateo's chin and brought his head down for kisses, wet and deep, full of all of his eager hopes, as he used his other hand to work open his own breeches. Releasing his prick, he shoved Mateo down to his knees.

Eyes dilated, body still trembling, Mateo didn't protest and Ópalo rubbed his thumb over Mateo's lower lip in anticipation. He jerked his hand rapidly over his cock, thinking of the future, feeling his heart beating for Mateo already, and shifting his adoring gaze between Mateo's liquid brown eyes and the sweet, red opening of his mouth. Lust ricocheted up and down his spine, making his feathers stand on end, and his heart beat bird-fast. Mateo thrust his tongue out between his lips, a flat, slippery surface that Ópalo couldn't resist.

He grabbed a handful of Mateo's hair and slid the head of his aching cock over Mateo's tongue, feeling the twitter of end-song in his blood and balls, rushing through his pelvis. Mateo's eyes snapped with a playful seductiveness as he flicked his tongue at the slit in Ópalo's cock head. Ópalo fought the urge to force Mateo's lips wider to shove into his waiting throat. Later, later.

Instead he threw his head back and sang

his pleasure and bright, new love as Mateo licked his sweet seed from where it leaked. As his feathers bristled, the song rushed harder through him. The music around them grew louder and louder, the sound of laughter, dancing, shouting and others achieving end-song seemed to swirl with Ópalo's own urgency. Mateo's lovely mouth was wide open, his eyes glazed with lust and his tongue out.

Ópalo crowed as he came, loud and raucous. Pink feathers exploded in his peripheral vision and his white, creamy seed burst onto Mateo's tongue. Mateo's eyes went wider and he squirmed. Ópalo held his hair tighter, decorating Mateo's cheeks, forehead and eyebrows with the slick of his release, delighted to see the evidence of his pleasure on his lover's face. Panting, shuddering, full of a sweet love and longing he'd been promised but never believed, he dropped to his knees. He wrapped his arm around Mateo's neck and licked the sweet fairy spendings from Mateo's stunned face.

"You're shaking," Ópalo said when they had both caught their breath.

"Am I?"

"Are you all right?"

"Oh, yes. I'm quite close to excellent, in fact."

Ópalo stroked a hand down Mateo's sweaty, spit-slick cheek, wiping away the dampness. Happiness whirled inside him as wild and beautiful as the dancing around him. "Come, let us dance. It's far from over."

Mateo nodded dumbly and stood when Ópalo did, following him out to the dance floor. Mateo's knees looked wobbly and his steps less refined, but before long the swing of the music and fairy madness overtook him again until they were kissing, rubbing, flying.

Chapter Six

THE DANCING WAS nothing like a ball at Mateo's court.

In the churning throng of barely restrained passion and primal desire, Mateo had been overcome by the lust in the air. If it had not seemed entirely fitting in the halls of the fae, his behavior would have embarrassed him beyond all ability to recover from it. As it was, he looked only at Ópalo as the music began to wind down—his blue eyes, his red lips, his feather-hair and his skin that in candlelight seemed to be made of a softer version of the stone for which he was named. Ópalo had done well for a distraction from the inappropriate behavior of Mateo's sisters.

Very well indeed.

Mateo had never imagined behaving so indecently—to taste and be tasted in public. Even though none had noticed, lost as they were to their own delirious lust, it still made him flush to remember how he'd been wanton as a whore.

Now with the dance over and his sisters flung over the shoulders of their fairy men and taken off to chambers within the castle of birdhouses, Mateo felt heat rise in his neck and face as he stared down at Ópalo's intense blue eyes.

"Come, *mi pájaro*," Ópalo murmured. "You could do with some air."

Mateo allowed Ópalo to lead him from the ballroom out onto a veranda overlooking the lake and bridge under which they'd rowed earlier in the day. It seemed a lifetime ago—and only moments, all at the same time.

The air off the water was refreshing on

Mateo's hot cheeks, and he leaned against the cool stone of the baluster, careful to keep his cloak in place. The moon was low in the sky. Somehow an entire day had passed as he'd watched the fae and their cousins swoop in revelry, and he had no idea how to gauge how much time had gone by at home.

His gut twisted at the thought, but then Ópalo was next to him, pointing out the birdhouse villages beyond the castle. Mateo's mind returned to the wonders around him, and all that he'd seen and done.

He thought of Ópalo's light, firm hand on his waist, commanding him through the dance, even as he'd gazed up from several inches down. Ópalo was small, but nothing about him was anything less than fierce. Even his kindness had an edge of strength that could not be denied.

"Are you well?" Ópalo asked, his voice like Pura's low-pitched, comforting coo.

"I am bedazzled," Mateo answered truthfully. "What I have seen today!" He gazed into Ópalo's eyes. "What I have learned and felt. I don't have words for it."

Lámina would probably have words for it, story upon story, tale upon tale, but none of them had prepared him for the fever-pitch delirium of the fae world. The sensuality would never have been appropriate for children's ears, and yet Mateo wished that Lámina had given some sort of hint. "I am bewildered."

Ópalo's lips quirked at the confession, and Mateo wondered if he should be embarrassed, but he wasn't. There was no loss of regard in Ópalo's amusement.

"What do we do now? How long does this last?"

"If you were to return now, perhaps an hour would have gone by in your world. Your sisters usually stay for three days and return in time for breakfast with your father."

Three days. Mateo felt a strange tug in his chest, like the lilting song of a morning bird, hopeful and new with optimism at the sight of the rising sun. "Three days here, in exchange for the time lost in a single night?"

"You sound so disbelieving. Is your world so lacking in magic that you can hardly imagine this is true?"

Mateo blinked at him. "Our world lacks any magic at all."

Ópalo seemed horrified by that thought. "None at all?"

"Not in the least."

"Your sisters had never mentioned that. Though I suppose I ought to have guessed, as delighted as they are by the smallest bit of magic. I always thought a little of our world must seep through to yours, and find myself saddened that it hasn't."

"Stories," Mateo said. "It comes through in stories."

Ópalo smiled. "Well, now you have three days to see the truth of those stories for yourself."

"And what are we to do during these three days? Something more than dance, surely. Though, given the state of my sisters' shoes when they return, I might be supposing too much."

Ópalo laughed. "There is plenty of dancing, yes, but Luz likes to row the lake and walk the gardens, talking to Azulejo about the books he reads her at night. Cielo and Blanca enjoy painting and archery. Adelita and Canario spend much time studying the maps, discussing politics and provinces. Diamante and Elisa play chess for hours, though I suspect it's merely an intellectual prelude to a different kind of game. Catalina and Halcón often swim, splash and fight. They are an odd couple, less suited than I might have thought, and yet they rut constantly."

"Stop." Mateo raised his hand. "I cannot hear this. My heart will never recover from such images."

"Then I shouldn't mention Gallo and Imelda. There's no dark corner that hasn't been graced by their amorous embrace.

Tulipan and Felipa ride out every morning and rarely return until night. They're enthralled with one another and seek only to be out of sight of other fae or human. Would you like to know of the others?"

Mateo knew he should care. But he found he didn't. "No. But tell me, what shall we do?"

"You intend to stay then? You don't wish me to row you back at once?"

Mateo gazed about, taking in the beautiful, strange world around him once more. How could he leave now? It seemed that he had only just stumbled onto a most marvelous discovery. "Yes. I will return with my sisters."

Ópalo's teeth, pressed into the pink pad of his lower lip, gleamed in the light of the moon. "I can't tell you how happy this makes me. As for how we spend your time here, I'll leave those choices to you, *mi pájaro*, until we discover what activities we enjoy."

Ópalo leaned against him, the heat of his

body drawing Mateo closer until their mouths were mere inches apart. "You've walked a great distance, seen too many new things and danced with great energy. It's time to rest."

Mateo licked his lips. He didn't wish to rest. His body felt alive, as though perhaps he had tasted fairy food. He thrummed and ached and wanted. A sweep of giddy emotion washed over him with an impulse to stand up on the edge of the balustrade and fling himself over to see if he, like Ópalo's vibrant cousins, could fly.

"My home…it seems far away. From this. Your world." Mateo gazed out at the water. Everything seemed so exciting, alive and marvelous.

The birdhouse villages shimmered on the horizon in colors Mateo had never imagined, and the fae themselves were shimmering, feathered beauties such as he'd never known possible. He thought of the village surrounding his father's castle, the dark, drab buildings, the grim stonework and the dirty villagers in their dingy clothes. Compared to Ópalo and his family, Mateo's father's and sisters' own garb seemed dull.

"What do you know of my world?" Mateo asked.

"Very little. Perhaps nothing in the scheme of things. I know that apples taste nice, but not as nice as your mouth."

Mateo laughed. "Nor as nice as yours."

"Indeed?"

"Indeed." Mateo took several more deep breaths and turned his back on the view, focusing on Ópalo's handsome face—the blue of his eyes, the marvel of his pink feathery eyebrows.

"You're certain of the passage of time?" Mateo had never known that blue eyes could be so warm, and he licked his lips, dropping his gaze to Ópalo's mouth.

"Quite sure."

"And staying does me no harm?" Mateo murmured.

"No harm at all. You're safe here. Relax and enjoy yourself."

"Tempting."

Ópalo indicated some side doors leading into the castle. "Come with me then?"

Mateo nodded, unable to find any reason to voice an objection, and let Ópalo lead him.

LIKE THE REST of the world into which Mateo had followed his sisters, Ópalo's chambers were strange and bizarrely beautiful. The ceiling was a domed mass of straw, sticks, and pieces of bright-colored threads woven into the fuzz of worn fabrics— an inverted nest. The internal walls were made of warm-colored materials and covered with brightly colored swaths of fabric, all frayed about the edges as though birds had pulled at the seams to extract threads for nests elsewhere—and Mateo believed they had, for the external wall was truncated with the top half open to the air.

A warm breeze wafted through the room, carrying the scent of the flowers he'd spotted on the veranda below, and the stars and moon were clearly visible in the night sky. To Mateo, who had lived through long, cold winters, the room was overwhelming in its beauty.

The chamber was sparsely decorated otherwise, with a wooden desk in the corner revealing a mess of what appeared to be plans or designs of some kind, an ornate armoire with the doors left open, revealing a spill of rich fabric and feathers within, and nothing else.

"Sleep will refresh you."

Ópalo motioned toward the pallet on the floor. Circular in shape, like the ceiling, it was more a nest than a bed, made of piles of colorful patterned blankets shot through with gold and silver threads, and plump cushions of such obvious softness that Mateo yearned to lie down on them, resting his weary body and propping up his sore feet. But sleep was something he didn't yet want.

He allowed himself to be maneuvered closer to the nest, his fingers shaking as he undressed himself, his eyes tracking Ópalo to the armoire.

"For you." Ópalo lifted a warm, brown nightshirt. "It may be small, but I'll have clothes made for you tomorrow, and this should do."

"No need. I prefer to sleep naked." If Mateo was in fairyland, then he intended to march bravely into debauchery. Too late to turn back now. "And as it stands, I don't want to sleep," Mateo said.

Ópalo's lips curved into a smile and he whispered, "Then we don't have to."

The nest was soft and warm. The pillows and blankets were smooth against Mateo's naked skin, and he felt safe lying on his back in its hollow while he watched Ópalo's clothes fall to the floor.

Mateo gripped his own cock, blood rushing hard as Ópalo threw his shirt aside, revealing a pale, sculpted chest and stomach with nipples so red they already looked kissed and bitten. Mateo moaned softly and licked his lips, eager to make them redder and harder, to tease them with his teeth and tongue.

As Ópalo's breeches dropped, Mateo's stomach curled with sharp desire and he gasped, jerking his cock slowly. He'd licked the head of Ópalo's prick, but he'd never imagined such beauty, such odd, fierce, strong beauty—solid and long, standing up in an eager hardness from a mat of pink feathers. And his balls! They looked so human and vulnerable within the wrinkled, tight walnut bulge of soft skin surrounded by the soft feathers above.

Mateo bit into his bottom lip, remembering the taste of the sweetness shot from them. He reached out to Ópalo, wanting him to kneel over Mateo's face so he could mouth his sac, grab that delicious-looking ass and thoroughly debauch himself in ways he'd only dreamed of before. While true friendship—or more—seemed impossible to fathom at the moment, there was no reason Mateo could think of now, resting comfortably as he was in Ópalo's nest, to hold back from his lusts. He'd yearned for a man's touch for years, and Ópalo had the skill and clear desire to share his own knowledge on the matter.

Yet Ópalo turned to the desk and opened one of its many drawers, withdrawing a bottle. Moonlight poured in, sparkling on the glass, lighting a path on the floor and dancing over Ópalo's skin.

"We'll need this," Ópalo said as he climbed into the nest.

Ópalo crawled toward him and Mateo reached to grab. Ópalo looked so light, as though his bones were hollow, and yet when he moved, it was with such strength that it took Mateo's breath away. Their kiss was not tentative, not even tender, but rough and full of want and promise. Mateo moaned for more of it, and as their hips surged together, pricks colliding again and again, they kissed and sucked, bit and whimpered, rolled, wrestled and struggled.

It was only when Mateo was pinned on his back, his right leg hitched up by one of Ópalo's arms, and Ópalo's slicked fingers pushed their way into his asshole that he realized in the midst of their passionate writhing and kissing, they'd been fighting for position—and he'd lost. Thank God he'd lost, for it was the sweetest defeat. He moaned as Ópalo's fingers breached him.

"Take me!"

"Shh," Ópalo soothed him, then nipped Mateo's earlobe. "Oh, I will take you."

Ópalo thrust his fingers in and out, and Mateo squirmed down, wanting more. It was all he'd wanted since he was old enough to know, all that no one had ever had the daring to take—being held down, being thrust into with fingers or cock, whatever they wished, calmed and stroked and mastered as he shook and begged for more. This, this had always been his dream—the secret things he'd longed for in the dark of his chambers.

"You're unused to this treatment, *mi pájaro*," Ópalo murmured. "You're so tight on my fingers."

"Please, please," Mateo begged, panting, his eyes stinging with sweat that dripped from his forehead, blurring his vision so that the ceiling became nothing but glinting color and light.

Ópalo's weight was firm against the back of Mateo's raised thigh. His fingers twisted inside Mateo until he found something. Mateo clenched his fists in the blankets under him, arched and made a sound he'd never made before—high pitched, unrestrained. And then Ópalo did it again. Mateo's balls drew up, his cock lifted and he almost shot his seed, but Ópalo shifted down to bite Mateo's lip hard, and instead of coming he cried out in surprise.

"Shush, now," Ópalo whispered, licking softly at the sore place he'd made on Mateo's lip. "Steady yourself. You're so handsome like this! All red lipped, hot skinned, and inside! You are so hot inside!"

Ópalo worked his fingers roughly over the place that made Mateo see flames behind his eyelids and set his asshole, prick and balls raging with need. The kisses Ópalo fed him now were gentle, full of nips and licks, but quite tender compared to Ópalo's treatment of his hole.

"Do you intend to drive me insane?"

"I intend to ready you."

"I believe you've done well enough of that," Mateo gasped.

"Do you? Perhaps you're right, *mi pája-ro.*"

When Ópalo slid his fingers out, Mateo almost grabbed Ópalo's hand to push them back inside, but Ópalo soothed him some more, and showed him the bottle.

"Let me slick myself," Ópalo whispered, and Mateo watched as the clear fluid in the bottle poured into Ópalo's palm. "Don't be afraid."

Glistening and ready, Ópalo's cock suddenly looked incredibly large, but Mateo was determined. "Do it. Now."

Ópalo's eyes were hot as blue fire as he grabbed Mateo's legs behind the knees, pushed them up with a strong grip and lined himself up. "Hold your legs open," Ópalo ordered, and Mateo obeyed, focusing on Ópalo's swollen lips, his burning eyes and his prick pushing for entrance at Mateo's hole.

The sharp burn that shot through his pelvis took his breath away. He squeezed his eyes shut as memories he'd nursed for years filled his mind—the smooth thrusts of the buggers he'd witnessed in the stables during his fourteenth year. He remembered the cries of pleasure, the body-shaking, howling end that had taken the impaled groom by storm and the milky seed that shot from his hard cock like cannon fodder.

This was not like this. This was pain. Where had the bliss from Ópalo's fingers run to? Now he felt as though his ass was being cleaved in half. He almost kicked Ópalo away. But Ópalo, in his surprising strength, took hold of his chin and forced Mateo to look up at him. "Do not take your eyes from my face."

Mateo stared at Ópalo, taking in his fierce commanding soul pouring into Mateo through his eyes. Mateo relaxed under his hand. As he did, Ópalo withdrew and then pushed inside again.

"That's it, *mi pájaro, sí. Sí.* So lovely, *muy guapo*, so tight and slick. That's it. Sweet, sweet bird. Sweet bird."

Ópalo moved against him, his stomach rubbing seductively against Mateo's cock, feathers tickling softly. Mateo relaxed more and more, and Ópalo's eyes grew hotter, and then it was good, deliciously good, and

Mateo reached between their bodies to grip his own prick.

"That's right. Touch yourself. Bring yourself pleasure. ¡*Sí*! Oh, Mateo! How good you feel around me!"

Mateo panted under Ópalo's rapid thrusts. He tried to keep his eyes on Ópalo's face, but couldn't for long, falling into a place where only the pleasure existed—his cock, his ass, Ópalo's prick slamming into him, the cries that sounded like desperate birdsong circling around them.

Then the world contracted, as though the room squeezed him tight. Ópalo pulled his cock out of Mateo's hole, jammed it back inside with much less care than the first time and collapsed onto Mateo, his hard, pale body fucking into him. Mateo's world exploded into pleasure, convulsing limbs, jerking pricks, spurts of wet seed, open mouths mashed together and too much ecstasy to comprehend.

It was more powerful than any climax

Mateo had known. All consuming and stuffed full with shuddering joy. And as he managed to open his eyes, panting and sweating from his exertions, he found himself holding Ópalo's shaking body tight against him while small, twittering cries of pleasure ripped from Ópalo's throat and pink feathers puffed from Ópalo's head and floated down around them. Mateo kissed Ópalo's temple, grinning at the tickle of feathers against his skin as they settled.

"And I haven't even tasted your heart yet," Ópalo whispered against Mateo's sweaty shoulder.

"God help me if you do," Mateo whispered.

His soul felt weak in the aftermath of pleasure. He was certain if Ópalo asked for his heart now and pressed a fairy cake to his lips, he'd eat it. The thought scared him, but not enough to move out of Ópalo's embrace or to regret a moment of what they'd done together. If anything, the rush of fear made him want to drown it out with more of Ópalo's skin, feathers, mouth and cock. Mateo squeezed around Ópalo's prick, still hard inside of him, and reveled in the madness.

Chapter Seven

ÓpALO SHIVERED AGAINST Mateo, remembering his own first experience of lying with another fairy. He'd been insatiable, wanting more of the fairy's cock, more of his kisses, more of everything, until he'd burned out bright and exhausted after a few days of near-constant pleasure. Ópalo hadn't felt that way since that first time, enjoying encounters well enough when he sought them out, but he'd always known he was meant for more. He was meant for Mateo.

Looking at Mateo's shining, sweaty form, still trembling around Ópalo's cock, he felt that same endless virility all over again. Mateo's hole spasmed against Ópalo's shaft, sending a surge through him, and Ópalo was tempted to roll his hips, thrust and start the pleasure all over again. He could ride Mateo's squirming, bucking body all night.

But he also sensed Mateo was inexperienced and he didn't wish to hurt him. Humans healed more slowly than fairies, his brothers had warned him after their own peerless first nights with Mateo's sisters.

"Was I too rough?" Ópalo asked softly, gently pulling his cock free and pressing his fingers to Mateo's hole.

"Put it back," Mateo commanded.

Ópalo snorted softly, lifting his head to smile at Mateo. "Eager for more?"

"Yes. Please, Ópalo. I want you back in me."

Ópalo mouthed at Mateo's shoulder, scraping his teeth against Mateo's hot skin. "I think not. After that, I must declare you are well and truly used, *mi pájaro*. You need rest."

"No, I'm fine. Ópalo, I'm ready. Truly. Let us do it again."

Ópalo smiled and touched Mateo's lips gently, feeling the dull thud of blood under their red, swollen skin. He obliged Mateo's begging by lining up his cock and pushing it back into Mateo's tight ass. "Better?" he asked.

"Mmm," Mateo answered, his eyelashes fluttering against his flushed cheeks.

Ópalo thrust gently, his own spendings smoothing the way. "One more time," he whispered, taking hold of Mateo's cock and pumping it gently.

It didn't take long. Mateo was relaxed and wanton, whining and moaning for more and harder, while Ópalo was gentle and slow, keeping his thrusts long and even. Mateo writhed against him, trying to speed his tempo, but Ópalo was determined not to break his human lover—certainly not on the first night.

"I need it," Mateo whimpered.

"I know you do. I'm giving it to you."

Mateo tossed his head, clenched around Ópalo's cock, grabbed handfuls of blankets and keened.

Ópalo grinned, keeping his thrusts steady and his hand moving on Mateo's straining cock. "There," he said, proudly. "There."

Mateo's face in ecstasy was beautiful—red cheeks, mouth blooming with cries, eyes wide and hot, staring into Ópalo's own. Then there was the tension in his muscles, wiry and strong. The animal beauty of his cock straining and finally pulsing once more with hard, strong kicks from his balls through his shaft. His pleasure wrenched him through a series of spasms that Ópalo captured in the clenching around his cock.

"*¡Dios mío!*" Mateo whimpered, dark curls sweaty against his face, his body heaving.

Ópalo pulled out of Mateo's ass, bent low to kiss it once as it spasmed and twitched closed, and then knelt over Mateo's form, moving his hand quickly along his own prick until he threw his head back and wrenched out drops of seed, singing to the rafters as he climaxed.

"Oh sweet fuck," Mateo cursed, watching him.

"Yes," Ópalo agreed, collapsing on top of Mateo, kissing his neck, his stubbly face and then his mouth.

They clung to each other, both trembling, until Mateo whispered, "I think I'm tired now."

Mateo fell asleep almost immediately, rolling away and curling onto his side, a sleep-smile on his lips, his face boyish in the moonlight. Ópalo turned his attention to the spendings smeared over both of them. He scratched at the drying clumps of it in his lower feathers before reaching out to run his fingers over the fresh seed on Mateo's hard stomach. He brought the white fluid to his lips. It tasted salty, different. Human.

Ópalo was tired too. Tired and a bit sore from the intensity of his end-songs. But sleep seemed an impossibility. He ran his eyes over Mateo's long limbs, sprinkled with dark hair—such an odd, soft and yet scratchy thing hair could be, so unlike feathers, and yet so lovely. Ópalo lingered at the matted tangle of tight curls around the base of Mateo's cock and admired the soft shape of it.

Bristles of hair also led from Mateo's cock up to his belly button, and Ópalo took another swipe of Mateo's seed from his stomach, licking it clean. Ópalo grinned, a thrill shooting through him. Mateo had arrived finally and was now naked and sated in his bed.

Oh Mateo. Mateo of the brown, wide eyes that seemed to grow ever darker as his lust grew, and then clenched close in a spasm of bliss as he came. Mateo, who made him feel as though his soul was flying. Ópalo felt as though he could rhapsodize over Mateo's handsome form forever, and yet—something was not quite as Ópalo had expected it to be. As happy as he was, he did not feel complete, not the way his siblings had described it to him after the arrival of their mates.

Ópalo fell back to the bed, examining the emptiness that dwelled somewhere beneath his rib cage. It was an ache he had a long acquaintance with.

"BUT IT DOESN'T feel right, Father," Ópalo said, sitting on his father's knee, watching the rest of his siblings learn the latest dances from the lovely Baila.

Every day his father oversaw the dancing. Aside from the guidance he gave to Canario with regard to the maps and some especially important alliances with fae from other kingdoms, dance was the only part of their education their father oversaw.

"Dance is a fairy's birthright," his father used to say. "To dance is to be fae. So you must learn to dance well, my darlings."

Soon Ópalo would join his siblings in the exhilarating lessons. He couldn't wait. The swinging movements that seemed to echo the flight of their cousins were intoxicating to watch and Ópalo wanted desperately to be part of it.

At his age, he was withheld from the great ballroom during the high dances, but one day he would be old enough and would join in. So he practiced daily with his siblings in their rooms, Azulejo being his most common partner. But sometimes Cacatúa swept him up and together they twirled about for hours.

"What doesn't feel right, *mi pájaro*?" his father asked, tugging on Ópalo's pink feathers affectionately.

"This hole in my heart." Ópalo put his small hand over his chest. "It doesn't hurt badly, Father, but only just. It cries out all the time for something to fill it."

"Ah." His father patted his head and frowned softly. "Unfortunately my boy, you must become accustomed to it. I'm afraid that ache in your heart won't be soothed for quite some time."

Baila spun Halcón around until he nearly tripped. Ópalo clapped when Halcón righted himself and began an even more difficult step, completing it with ease. Halcón sneered at Ópalo, rebuffing his childish enthusiasm as he always did, but his sneer slipped when their father lifted a hand in his direction.

"Never mind him, Ópalo. He misses his mother."

Ópalo never understood what that per-ennial excuse for Halcón's dislike had to do with him, but he was accustomed to it, and the world would not seem right without Halcón's glares and sneers.

"Do you have it too, Father?"

"What? Oh, the hole? I do. Mine never went away. Not with their mother, and not with yours. I'm afraid a human heart is the only remedy, and there was never a human heart meant for me. My father's alliance with the humans was broken." His father tapped Ópalo's nose with the end of a long gray feather. It had fallen from his father's head at the beginning of the lesson when Baila had used Father as a partner to demonstrate a step. Since then, they had taken turns tickling each other with it. "But that is where you are lucky, Ópalo. You have a human heart and a human bride waiting for you. I have seen to it. And when she arrives, the ache will be gone. All you must do is grow up and be patient. Do you think you can do that?"

"I can try, Father."

Baila and Cacatúa were taking their turn now, and Ópalo watched them spin. The blur of their skirts was dizzying, and when they both set their heels down in time, striking a pose together, Ópalo smiled and clapped with giddy joy.

Father patted him. "That's my good little bird."

ÓPALO SIGHED, TURNING back to study Mateo's dark lashes resting on his golden cheek. Patient, his father had said, was all Ópalo had to be. Ópalo was unusually good at cultivating patience. His work called for it, and dealing with all of his brothers and his sister required it. Then there was the matter of waiting for Mateo to come. So long he'd waited. Not as many years as Canario or any of the older siblings, but long enough that he was eager now for the ache to end.

But now it seemed he must wait even longer, because Mateo did not yet return his devotion. The choice to warn him against the fairy food seemed foolish in the light of Mateo's beautiful body and the pleasure they'd shared—and especially when measured against the continued ache in Ópalo's chest.

Perhaps his siblings had been right to take the shorter approach, bypassing whatever a human might require before falling in love under the power of fairy magic. Because now that Mateo was here, Ópalo didn't know just how patient he could continue to be.

Exhaustion began to overwhelm his excitement, and he curled up next to Mateo, taking in the scent of his skin and the warmth of his breath. Ópalo started to drift off, his hand wrapped around Mateo's forearm, brushing softly against the hair his fingers found there. He reminded himself that he had three days, after all. Surely Mateo would love him by then? And if he did not, then perhaps when he returned....

Ópalo jolted awake. His next thought so terrible that his heart pounded in his chest, and his skin went clammy with fearful sweat.

What if Mateo leaves with his sisters and

never returns?

Ópalo rose from the bed and paced, watching the moon traverse the sky, wondering at his own stupidity in not taking the easy way.

Chapter Eight

MORNING OPENED WITH a symphony of birdsong and Mateo stretched luxuriously, reveling in the heavy relaxation in his limbs. His lower back felt loose and warm, and he knew if he opened his eyes, he wouldn't find himself in his room at the castle. Instead he was naked in the nest of a fairy with whom he'd shamelessly shared carnal delights. He kept his eyes closed, prolonging the moment before he faced a world in which fairies truly existed and his sisters were as good as married.

When Mateo was ready, he found the room a brighter version of what he'd seen the night before. The light from the morning sun sparkled in the golden threads throughout the ceiling nest above and reflected off a mirror hanging next to the armoire. He heard the cry of a bird just before one soared into the room, tore a long length from a red piece of fabric hanging on the wall opposite, and flew out again.

Slowly, he turned onto his side to face the naked, curled form of the fairy next to him. As he met Ópalo's intent gaze, a wave of heat flooded Mateo's belly and chest, rose up his neck and warmed his cheeks. It wasn't shame or even embarrassment at what they'd done, but it was a shyness that took him by surprise, a bashful sort of joy he'd never felt before.

"Hello," Ópalo said softly. "Did you sleep well?"

"I did. And you?"

"You snore," Ópalo said by way of answering. A grin dimpled his cheeks. "Has anyone ever told you?"

"No, I didn't know."

"It's a funny-sounding snore, with a whistle at the end."

"My apologies. It must have kept you awake."

Ópalo's eyes softened and he tilted his head against the pillow. "No, it was my pleasure to listen to your hideous night noises." He laughed and propped his head on his hand.

Mateo sat up, pink feathers sticking to his skin. The bed was littered with them. He remembered puffs of molted color when Ópalo had reached climax, and Mateo plucked one off his thigh and studied it. The stem was a deeper pink than the barbs, almost red, and the downy part at the bottom was so light it was nearly white.

"I enjoyed last night," Mateo said, keeping his gaze on the feather.

"As did I."

"And at home, it's still the middle of the night?"

"Yes, in your world they'll sleep for days yet."

Mateo twirled the feather. "I must decide what I intend to do."

Ópalo bolted up beside him. "About?"

"About my sisters and their marriages." He looked to Ópalo, raked his eyes over Ópalo's mouth, his long neck and his firm chest. He dragged his gaze back up before he lost his train of thought contemplating Ópalo's hard cock. At the edge of his peripheral vision, he could see how the rosy head of it pressed against Ópalo's stomach. Mateo swallowed hard. "About you."

"Do you want to decide before or after breakfast?" Ópalo asked.

Mateo frowned. "You told me not to eat."

"My breakfast," he clarified. "I'm famished."

Mateo watched Ópalo rise from the bed, his cock swinging in midair, proud and erect.

"Do you mind?" Ópalo asked. "I'll call

for them to bring me something, and then I'll happily listen as you decide what to do about your sisters and their marriages. What you decide to do about me."

Mateo nodded dumbly, unable to speak around the lust rising through him. His own cock lengthened and strained for Ópalo's attention. He rubbed a hand over his face, trying to concentrate. He'd been thinking about the situation with his sisters, about the fae and the prospects for marriage.

Ópalo let out a loud call, and birds echoed it from outside. He grabbed a red sheet from the pile of fabric spilling from the armoire and wrapped it around his waist, accentuating his pale skin, bright nipples, red mouth and pink hair. Mateo swallowed hard. He'd never known he could be so moved by these particular details of a man's body. He'd been aroused by Sir Franco's forearms and broad chest, and there had been others fair of face and strong of shoulder, but red nipples had never entered his mind as being the apparent aphrodisiac that they were.

It's because he's fae. It's the power I sense from him, some kind of fairy thrall and nothing more.

And yet, he found he didn't care.

Ópalo seated himself at the edge of the nest, smiling. "Go on then?"

Mateo's cock was insistent now, fairy thrall or no, he wanted to rub his hard length all along Ópalo's neck, down his chest, over his trail of feathers and then squeeze it up next to Ópalo's cock. "I'm afraid I can't think."

Ópalo shrugged one shoulder and said, "Would you like me to suck you while we wait for my food?"

Mateo said nothing. He was so desperately aroused that falling back on the bed and spreading his legs was all that he could manage.

ÓPALO WAS ACCUSTOMED to keeping his silence while other people worked through issues and made plans he might not agree with. He never would have survived his childhood with eleven older siblings had he not. Yet with Mateo he found it harder than usual not to interject.

Perched side by side on the edge of the nest, they faced the window. Ópalo listened as Mateo ruminated. He spread nectar over his morning boiled eggs, a combination that made Mateo cock his head curiously. Ópalo almost offered up a bite, but then remembered with regret that Mateo would not be eating during his time here.

"I should reveal myself to my sisters," Mateo said thoughtfully, running long, handsome fingers through his soft curls.

Ópalo popped several berries into his

mouth, enjoying the combination of flavors. "What will they think when they see you?"

"I'm sure they'll at first believe me here to thwart their happiness."

"Isn't that why you came?"

"Hardly. I came because I wanted to discover their secret and put a stop to whatever it was they were doing that's causing my father so much distress. He has an old heart, you see. He can't be expected to live much longer under the strain they've put him under."

"So your aim was to thwart their happiness for a noble cause."

Mateo frowned and leaned forward to put his elbows on his knees, gripping his hair in both hands. "I had no idea what I would find. It isn't as though I could have known fairyland was real, that fae exist and that my sisters have given themselves over willingly to them."

"As have you."

Mateo scoffed. "My body perhaps. My

heart is still my own."

Ópalo hid his flinch and busied himself with adding more nectar to his eggs. The hole in his own heart throbbed at Mateo's careless reminder. *He doesn't know what it means for you. Don't think him callous.* Ópalo took a steadying drink of water and met Mateo's eyes again, listening.

"Their hearts have been given away utterly. I can see that for myself. It explains everything. Their behavior toward our father, the cold reaction to my pleas that they stop before they kill him. The fae have their hearts now. Their souls."

"You seem under the misapprehension that my siblings are somehow controlling your sisters. They choose for themselves, *mi pájaro.* Out of love for your father they return to your world. They could easily have chosen to stay."

Mateo stared at Ópalo, seeming to measure the veracity of his statements. "Why haven't they been honest with him then?"

Ópalo shrugged and popped egg into his mouth. "I imagine it's out of fear that the truth will kill him, or he'll somehow stop them from coming. He could block off the portal, or destroy it entirely. It's a risk they've been unwilling to take."

"They should have been honest. At least with me."

"Luz was considering it and I was hopeful she would since I'd begun to dream you might be the bride."

"I'm no one's bride."

"I've been waiting for you." Ópalo didn't point out that Mateo had shared his bed quite willingly and that save for Ópalo's inopportune fall into love and subsequent decision to forego the fairy cakes during their row on the lake, Mateo would be his bride—happily so.

"Yet she didn't tell me. She left me to discover it all for myself. I would have expected my twin to take me into her confidence and allow me to enter this world more prepared."

"Prepared with what?" Ópalo lifted his brow and made the mocking motion of shooting a bow. "An army perhaps?"

Mateo shifted guiltily. "It isn't as though we are a martial people. Father and I, had we understood the full extent of their dedication to their lovers, would have come to a reasonable conclusion, I'm certain. We wouldn't have hurt you."

"We fae are peaceful unless provoked. Then we are quite dangerous. We have magic, our cousins' claws and beaks, and an arsenal of fairy weapons on our side. Perhaps your sisters wanted to forestall any possibility of outright conflict. Because if my siblings felt their brides were threatened, rest assured, they would hurt you."

As I will hurt anyone or anything that tries to bring harm to you, mi pájaro.

Mateo's jaw worked and his gaze turned to the open wall. The sky was incredibly blue and the clouds were white spires in the air.

The cousins darted about playing games of chase.

Mateo sighed. "It's complicated. I can see that now."

"Perhaps your sisters simply hadn't had time to figure out an elegant resolution to the problem."

Mateo laughed, but it wasn't a pretty sound like the sweet giggles and chuckles Ópalo had elicited from him earlier in the nest. "Hardly. I rather believe that in the end they found a great deal of amusement in fooling everyone, in proving they were smarter than all those silly suitors. Smarter than all of us."

"Suitors?"

"Didn't they tell you? I suppose they wouldn't for fear you might not allow them to go back. My father is even now running a contest, one might call it. Whosoever can tell him where my sisters go at night and what they do there will win the hand of any of my father's children and the riches to go with it."

"Any of his children?"

"That's right. Even me. My sisters' shenanigans have put my future and my happiness on the gaming table. I think you begin to understand why I feel they owed me an explanation."

Ópalo could indeed. "Were there any contestants for your hand?"

Mateo's brow arched and his red lips quirked. "Why? Would you like to compete?"

Ópalo swallowed another bite of egg rather than replying. The idea of going up against a human for Mateo made his heart pound with a bloodthirsty thrill he'd never experienced. His feathers twisted on his head, and he felt a cold sensation sweep over him. He'd win if it came to physical combat. He was small, but he was fierce, and he wasn't going to let Mateo just walk away with some hot-blooded brute of a human.

"You'd be going up against a princess who hopelessly loves my sister Adelita and an old widowed king who wants to build me the biggest dovecote I've ever seen in exchange for me being sweet about sucking his prick."

Ópalo's feathers settled again. The odds of winning should it come to confronting these opponents had gone from certain to dead certain, and he no longer felt the urge to shred his napkin. "Do you want either of them?"

Mateo's laughter was genuine this time. "I say not. I gather you understand the princess lacks a certain something I'd sorely miss, and the king…well, I think I made myself clear of my opinion of him in my original description of his Highness."

"Then I see no reason to compete. I'm incontestable."

Mateo snorted. "Overconfident, I'd say."

"Would you?"

"Indeed. If I had to choose between you and one of them, I'd choose you of course," Mateo said, but his tone was not exactly encouraging. "Still I'd rather not be forced to choose at all. I don't intend to marry. I'll win my own hand from my father and do as I see fit with my life."

Ópalo's chest felt tight. He couldn't stop his mind from turning back to what they'd shared in the nest—pleasure, sweat, laughter, cries of ecstasy—and wondering how Mateo could make it sound as though choosing Ópalo would be such a disappointment.

Ópalo cleared his throat. "So you will reveal your sisters' secret to your father?"

Mateo nodded. "I will. I'm not quite sure when or how just yet. But I'll reveal it to him once I've determined whether or not arrangements for their marriages to your siblings are something I can condone." Then his face softened. "And when I'm quite sure that the portal won't be damaged or destroyed. Because I don't believe I'm done playing with you just yet."

Ópalo licked his spoon clean of nectar, keeping his eyes averted. He'd always been so sure of himself, and Mateo's casual disregard for the hole in Ópalo's heart and the call of their fate was an unexpected bludgeon to his confidence. Yet Mateo didn't seem to mean any harm by it. He spoke like it was perfectly natural and as if Ópalo couldn't possibly feel any more strongly for him that he felt for Ópalo.

Humans were so oddly protective of their hearts when not under the sway of fairy magic. He wondered if their world made it so, or if it was a defect in Mateo alone. Perhaps this reluctance in him was what had held the brides back for so long. Perhaps this was why Lámina had not sent them before.

"I am not done with you either," Ópalo said, putting his napkin and spoon aside. "The cousins have no doubt delivered the message to the tailor with your measurements by now and fresh clothes should arrive within the hour. We should spend that time in my nest, don't you think? I believe there is a position you'll enjoy."

Mateo's cheeks flamed, and yet he

crawled back into Ópalo's nest before Ópalo even stood to drop his feathered robe to the floor.

Chapter Nine

L UZ'S DARK HAIR splayed out in the green grass where she lay next to the blue-feathered fairy Mateo had seen her with the night before. She wore a grand dress constructed of purple and green feathers. Though Mateo rarely paid much attention to the fashion of the *damas de corte* or his sisters, he recognized that it was unlike any gown she owned back home.

As Mateo approached with Ópalo's hand at the small of his back, his stomach tightened. Certainly it was time to confront his sisters, starting with Luz, and let them know of his presence in fairyland. But would she be able to look at him and know that he'd spent the night and morning in Ópalo's nest, held down and mounted?

For all the teasing Luz and his other sisters had given him over the years, his experience with Ópalo was too private and still far too raw to be the subject of his twin's amusement. He could feel the control he'd been seeking over his older sisters—yes, nine minutes made a difference—flying from him like the birds that scattered from the edge of the lake at his approach.

Luz twirled a flower in her fingers and laughed at something the fairy next to her said before taking note of the birds' flight and turning her head. Mateo barely had time to work his mouth into the form of a greeting when Luz was up and barreling toward him, charging into him with a grin and a hug so fierce he took several steps back, accidentally knocking Ópalo to the ground.

"Little brother!" she cried, kissing his cheek and clutching at the bright-green jacket Ópalo's tailors had constructed for him so quickly that fairy magic must have been involved. "I knew it was you following us in the forest!"

Mateo blinked rapidly. He'd been so certain of his own stealth. "You knew? How?"

"Your cologne, silly. But never mind now. Tell me, how did you do it?"

Out of the corner of his eye, Mateo saw his sister's fairy help Ópalo up, and felt certain that he'd failed to be gallant in some important way. But Ópalo was grinning as he knocked the dirt from the seat of his breeches and didn't seem offended by Mateo's distraction from offering him a gentlemanly hand.

"How did you follow us without being seen? You, who could never win at hide-and-seek, managed to fool Adelita and all the rest!"

"Lámina gave me a magic cloak. It makes me invisible."

It was absurd when he said it aloud, but Luz accepted it easily enough. Why shouldn't she? They were in fairyland, keeping company with fae. What was so amazing about a magic cloak in comparison to that?

"An invisible cloak! How wonderful." She laughed. "Oh Mateo. I'm so glad you're here. Is it not marvelous? Is it not beautiful?" Luz gripped his arms and shook him slightly. "Aren't you happy I didn't make a scene in the forest and reveal you to Adelita then? Though what would she have done, really? Made you wait there for our return? Hardly. You're happy to be the final bride! I knew it!"

"You didn't know anything," Mateo said, sounding ridiculous to his ears. Now was not the time to be childish. Still, there was comfort in the ritual of their teasing. Amidst the madness of nests, bird cousins and fae that seduced humans beyond caring, it was nice to know that Luz was still going to take credit for all of his accomplishments, and he was still going to dispute it.

"Don't I though?" Luz reached up and rumpled his hair. "You look well-tumbled if I do say so myself. Is it not wonderful? Is it not all the poets said it would be and more?"

Mateo's cheeks went hot, but he narrowed his eyes at her. His feelings on the matter of his couplings with Ópalo were jumbled and he didn't intend to share any of his confusion with Luz. A few months ago, when their relationship had still been open and honest, he would have gone to her eagerly, hopeful she could help him put his thoughts to right. Now after all her deceit and knowing full well the extent of her own commitment to the fae, how could he trust her with the intimacy of his pleasure and Ópalo's strange and poorly concealed expectations?

"I would say by the state of him and my brother's expression that well-tumbled is an understatement. Well done, brother," the blue-green fairy said with a wicked twinkle in his eye. "You were always a patient one and an overachiever in the arts of dance and defense. It should not surprise me you'd perform well in the nest too."

Given what the fairy had no doubt done to his sister—and with the aid of fairy aphrodisiacs no less—Mateo bristled at this easy discussion of his private intimacies.

"I don't believe this is a topic we need to discuss," Ópalo began.

But Mateo drew himself up, pushed Luz aside and stepped close enough to the other fairy to be intimidating. He felt the tug of Luz's hand on his arm and Ópalo's fingers close around his other wrist.

"I don't believe I know your name."

"Azulejo. I am at your service." The fairy's eyes darted to Ópalo, apology evident there, but to Mateo's mind directed at the wrong person.

Mateo studied Azulejo's face, not backing down. Finally, with a slow, even tone, he bit out, "So you're the man who took my sister's heart."

"Is that such a bad thing?"

"Yes, when you didn't even allow her to freely choose, and instead fed her enchanted cakes."

"Mateo," Luz said sharply. "I made my choice. Quite freely."

He ignored her, jerking free of Ópalo's hold and stepping close enough to Azulejo to see the blue feathers of his eyebrows ruffle.

"You didn't offer him cakes?" Azulejo asked Ópalo, not tearing his eyes from Mateo's face. "Are you really such a fool?"

"Azulejo," Ópalo warned.

"Never mind. Apparently you are. I wish I could claim surprise, but you always did go your own way. It makes Halcón crazy, but oh well, brother, I suppose it must make life interesting."

"Don't act as though I'm not here," Mateo said. "It is me you should be addressing. Look me in the eye or else."

"Do you threaten me?" Azulejo asked, amusement tinting his vibrant voice. "You intend to take us all on, then? We're vicious fighters, I should warn you. All claws and sharp beaks."

Mateo felt a wave of uncertainty swell inside his chest. No fae had beaks that he had seen, but Ópalo had spoken of their magic and their arsenal.

"Azul!" Ópalo's voice now held a razor's note.

Mateo did not look away from Azulejo's smug face.

Azulejo broke first, bowing deeply, the feathers at the crown of his head brushing against Mateo's chest as he swooped down and then back up again. "As you wish, little brother." He lifted a feathered brow at Mateo. "Our strength shouldn't be underestimated, but I forgive you. You've had quite a shock."

Mateo flared his nostrils, and Ópalo chose that moment to wriggle between them, his pink feathers tickling the underside of Mateo's chin.

"Azulejo is closest to my age, enjoys singing, dancing, writing poetry and making a mess out of the statesman duties our elder brothers assign him," Ópalo spoke in a rush, his voice quivering with tension. "You'll like him if you only give him a chance."

"And control your temper, baby brother," Luz said.

Mateo snorted. "Nine minutes!"

"Nine minutes means nothing at all," she said. "But before long, you'll meet the others, and Azulejo is a darling compared to Halcón, who will sooner rip your throat out and deal with Ópalo's displeasure after than bear any disrespect!"

Ópalo actually moved against Mateo in a way that could only be described as protective at the mention of Halcón's name. Mateo gently pushed him aside, squaring his shoulders. He didn't need protection. Or at least he didn't want to appear as if he needed any. Not in front of Luz, at any rate. She'd only tease him mercifully later when he was least expecting it.

Assuming I don't murder her and all my sisters for getting us into this predicament to begin with. Why could they not have been happy at home?

Mateo remembered the hours in Ópalo's nest and knew the answer to that, whether he liked it or not. How could being locked up in their father's castle compare to this paradise?

"*Tu novio* is feisty, brother," Azulejo said with a smile that still put Mateo's teeth on edge. "I like him. So much more your style than any delicate *mujer*. It truly explains much. So…" Azulejo said, stepping back from Mateo, breaking the tension. "What took you so long? My brother has waited for months."

Mateo said nothing, noting how Luz wrapped her arm through Azulejo's and smiled up like he was the sun and she was a flower who would follow him across the sky. He'd never seen Luz look at any man that way.

If Ópalo had been different, if he'd fed me, would I be like her? Lost to him and desperately in love?

Even now he was under the influence of a more subtle fairy thrall, and while he didn't wish to break it for the time being, he wasn't fool enough to believe it was real.

"A man must make his own way," Ópalo said, his chin up and his eyes bright. "There's no shame in taking the long route."

"You always had more patience than any of the rest of us, Ópalo." Azulejo laughed before plopping down on the grass again, patting the spot next to Luz after she followed him down. "Place your shameless selves here and enjoy the day with us. Tonight's dance will begin soon enough, and then the long gratifying night. We'll require rest to fully enjoy pleasure."

"Please sit, Mateo," Luz said. Her voice reflected an uncertainty that relieved Mateo's mind. At least she seemed to realize now that something was different with him than it was with her and the others.

After a few awkward moments of silence upon the grass, the twitter of birds the only noise and Luz's concerned glances the only eye contact, Ópalo and Azulejo began to discuss plans for the night's festivities.

Luz scooted closer to Mateo and ducked her head to catch his eye. "Why are you angry, Mateo?"

"Can you truly not guess the answer to that? For weeks, no, months you've lied to me, to Father, and brought his health near to breaking. Not to mention nearly traded my hand to that beastly King Hernando!"

"We never would have allowed that."

"Why? Because you're all so very smart and your schemes entirely foolproof? What if Hernando had not taken your drugged wine?"

"But he did."

Mateo glared at her.

"What? Mateo, come now. He did take the wine. They always do."

"Just as you took the food offered you here and now you are trapped. But you don't even see it, believing yourself in love when all you are is enchanted."

Luz shook her head. "Trapped? Here? I know what I feel. I know the joy it brings me, the freedom. We are all so very happy." She sounded even more confident as she went on. "Look at Imelda! Who in our world would ever want her crass mouth? Here Gallo laughs heartily at all of her wicked jokes."

"Your happiness isn't real, Luz. Don't you see?"

"We weren't forced, Mateo. We ate willingly."

"You knew the price before the first bite? That you must return to fairyland forever or suffer? That you would then feel...that the fairy thrall would cause you..." He motioned with his hand trying to indicate the aphrodisiac effect. "You knew all of that and still chose?"

"Yes." Luz spoke truly, her gaze unwavering. "We knew. We were ready to become the women we are meant to be. As soon as we crossed the portal we knew our fate was at hand. Do you not…can you not feel it?" She frowned. "It is as Lámina foretold. Surely for you as well?

"I don't know. I wish I did."

Luz went on in a rush. "But Lámina knew, Mateo. Lámina sent us. She sent you as well." Her eyes lit up. "Oh! Here!" she reached into a nearby basket and pulled forth a small iced fairy cake, intricately decorated. "If you eat just a little, you'll see and you'll be happy too."

Mateo stared at the shiny cake. It would surely taste of every sugary, heavenly thing that had ever passed between his lips. His fingers itched to take it from her, and he licked his mouth in anticipation.

Suddenly the cake was dashed from her hand onto the grass.

"No," Ópalo said, leaning over from where he sat next to Azulejo. "I promised he would not be influenced. He is uncertain still, while you and your sisters never hesitated." His pale face was set, as though it pained him to say the words, but he didn't waver. "Mateo alone will decide if he ever eats of fairyland."

Azulejo let out a low whistle of disapproval, and previously unseen birds took flight from the field around them, cawing what sounded to Mateo's ears a message of censure.

"Oh," Luz replied, surprise looking pretty on her, as nearly every emotion did. "I see."

I could snatch it up even now and eat it.

The thought was similar to his urge to climb upon the balustrade the night before—against every fiber of his being, but somehow exciting. He resisted.

"Then you haven't decided what you plan to do, Mateo? About us? About father?"

Mateo pulled his eyes away from the discarded fairy cake. "It seems there's nothing for it but to convince Father to allow you to marry your fairy lovers."

"Oh thank you!" Luz cried, throwing her arms around him. He held her and smelled her hair. He realized that the new scent he'd noticed on her recently was not a new perfume, but fairyland itself.

He whispered in her ear, "For who else will have you now?"

Luz pulled back, dark eyes hot with anger. She seemed about ready to slap his face, which Mateo almost welcomed. He still felt she and the others deserved a good shouting at, but he turned to Azulejo and asked with every appearance of making a genuine effort, "So, you dance every night?"

"Only the nights our brides are present," Azulejo said.

Mateo was ready to protest the description of his sisters—and especially himself—as brides, when Ópalo took hold of his hand. His fingers were smooth and cool.

"Now that's settled," Ópalo said softly.

"Why don't you come with me to visit our dove cousins, Mateo? There'll be time for making friends with Azul later."

"Oh yes, Mateo, you should go," Luz said. "You've never seen the like. Ópalo showed me their dovecote several visits ago and even then I longed for you to see it."

Mateo agreed, since further discussion of their situation was only going to bring up sticking points such as his sisters' enchanted state, their deceit and lies, the danger to their father's health and Mateo's unresolved anger about the situation.

Luz kissed his cheek and whispered in his ear, "Please Mateo, give it time. You could be so happy here with us if you would only let yourself."

Mateo imagined that was true. The pleasure he engaged in with Ópalo was not without joy. But he had no intention of surrendering his heart, just as he'd no intention of surrendering his hand to Hernando.

"We'll see you at dinner," Ópalo said, nodding to Luz and Azulejo.

"Enjoy your first day as a married fairy," Azulejo said, winking. "Or should I say as the fairy thrall of a reluctant human, since you didn't feed him properly."

Ópalo rolled his eyes and wordlessly slipped his arm around Mateo's back, guiding him away from Luz and Azulejo.

Chapter Ten

"WHERE IS THIS dovecote?" Mateo asked, the vibrant flowers and verdant grass around him both familiar and yet fresh to his eyes.

"You can see it from here." Ópalo pointed toward a wide tower of birdhouses Mateo could just glimpse on the horizon, soaring up to the bright white clouds.

As they walked, Ópalo began to talk. "Azulejo is a good fairy, Mateo. He's kind, joyful, funny and loving. He's stood up for me many times, even in the face of some heavy opposition from our older brothers."

"Not your sister?"

"I've always been Cacatúa's pet. But my brothers, well, they are a story for another day. Let me assure you Luz is in good hands. I understand you're uncertain of what has transpired, but you must admit she seems well."

Mateo couldn't deny it.

"Give some leeway to the fact that our world doesn't share the same morality as yours. We're open, high-flying children of the sun and the sky, the cousins of birds. We don't dress out of modesty, but out of a joy in the colors with which we can decorate ourselves. Our knowledge of goodness is pleasure, peace, laughter, joy. Here, what Azulejo and your sister have shared is celebrated and honored, no matter the enchantments their love was first built upon."

Mateo's head reeled. It was all too much to take in. He began to wish he'd never left Ópalo's nest. Sleeping off his night of indulgence would have been a better thing for him surely than tramping through an unfamiliar landscape and challenging his sister's lover. Perhaps he should simply give his sisters a blessing. Their lovers were royalty after all, and happiness shone brightly on Luz's face, marred only by his own apparent buffoonery in the face of what he didn't understand.

They walked in silence until they closed in on the towering structure of elaborate, stacked birdhouses. Doves swooped and called as they approached and Ópalo waved as if to old friends. "This dovecote was constructed over the course of a hundred years and we still add to it today as our population of doves grows."

"This is…they are magnificent," Mateo said. "I have a dovecote at home and I've considered investing in a much larger one, but I've never imagined, much less seen, such an amazing structure."

"The view from the top is the most lovely in our land."

"We are to climb?"

Ópalo looked up at the tower of birdhouses and frowned. After a long moment he turned his gaze back to Mateo and laughed. "I suppose not, *mi pájaro*. Big, strong human that you are, you might pull it down on top of us. Wouldn't that be a waste of a hundred years' labor!" This last was spoken with a playful trill that Mateo felt in his gut, and he wanted to jerk Ópalo close and kiss him.

Ópalo smiled, raising a hand for a large dove to light upon. "We take the homes of our cousins quite seriously. You should see where the crows live. If you stand at the highest point of the castle at dawn, you can see it to the east with the sun reflecting off all its stolen, shiny baubles."

The dove on Ópalo's wrist cooed and ducked her head to better examine Mateo.

"She reminds me of Pura," Mateo said, looking at the bird's beautiful gray feathers. "My favorite dove at home."

"She likes you. She thinks you're handsome. And kind."

"She can tell that much by looking?"

Ópalo's brows lifted as he considered the dove's expression. "You'd be rather surprised what the cousins can see."

"I always trust my doves' opinions of people," Mateo admitted. "Pura knew that King Hernando was a prig. She flicked her wings at the sight of him and tried to take a piece out of his finger, though he thought she was after his crust of bread." He chuckled, remembering. Mateo's father had not found it so funny.

"King Hernando?"

"The old, unattractive man who smells of cabbage and who is at this moment snoring on the floor of my sisters' chambers, no doubt absorbed in dreams of winning my hand and gaining my mouth on his prick."

Ópalo's feathers seemed to bristle on the crown of his head and the dove clicked before she took flight from them. They stared after her together. "You've been close enough to the man to smell him?"

Mateo couldn't miss the thread of anxiety behind Ópalo's demeanor. "Unfortunately."

Ópalo took his chin. "Has he ever touched you?" Ópalo's eyes were not laughing.

Mateo chuckled softly. "Are you jealous? He touched my cheek, devised a reason to rub his thumb over my lip and took my hand on more than one occasion."

Ópalo made an animal noise, growling low. "Never again," Ópalo said softly, his eyes lingering on Mateo's mouth. "You're with me now."

"Oh, am I?" Mateo laughed.

Ópalo's lips twisted down at the edges, as though Mateo had questioned something essential to his understanding of the world. "Of course you are."

Doves flew down from the tower above and landed in the dirt beside them. Mateo felt their eyes on him, and he suddenly remembered a man on trial in his father's court, standing before the tribunal of men who would decide his destiny. *Will they tear me apart if I reject him?*

"I daresay I'm not. I barely know you."

"You know enough."

"While it's true that what I do know I'm enamored of, I fear these feelings are based in something not entirely real."

Ópalo looked queasy. The birds clicked and made barking noises of agitation.

Mateo swallowed against the odd sense that he was telling a lie, even though every word he said was true.

"This is real. And I believe you will choose it. You will choose me." Ópalo's hands shook, but he seemed convinced of his own words.

The shimmer of Ópalo's eyes pulled at Mateo. He felt rather convinced himself, which was deliriously ridiculous and deliciously reassuring all at once. Still, he couldn't keep his mind from supplying an argument. "For all your talk of choice, telling me not to eat the fairy cakes so I can be completely free to come and go as I like, where is your own choice in all of this?"

"What do you mean?"

"Only that you've waited for your 'bride' your whole life, and now that I've arrived, you've accepted me without a second thought. How can you be so certain I'm the man for you? You might not even like me once you've known me more than a day or two."

Ópalo stared at Mateo as though he'd just grown a second head. His pink feathers bristled and shifted, puffing slightly as though his inner irritation was pushing up through to the surface. "It's the way it is. How it always will be, Mateo. Didn't Lámina explain it to you?"

You love the fae. You always love them and they always love you. It is how it is. It is how it shall be.

Mateo had to admit he already felt a

strong compulsion to be near Ópalo, but was that love? Or the natural consequence of the shared pleasure they'd taken together? Pleasure that Mateo, without a doubt, strongly desired to share again. It was possible he wanted that more than anything else in his life, but should their passion wear away, would he even like Ópalo? His gut told him yes, and his heart seemed to agree. Yet his head was unwilling to commit.

Ópalo lifted his hands as though to present himself. "I am Ópalo, the youngest of the twelve fae. I am the fairy meant for you." He seemed confident but also vaguely horrified, as if he also felt that his own existence and reason for being were on trial between them, and Mateo's judgment would justify or extinguish him.

Mateo had no idea what to say. Ópalo was handsome, fascinating and terribly confusing, but he could not say he felt they were designed for each other. They'd only just met.

"I'm apparently the human made for you, but if you're asking for my hand or some sort of commitment in the form of eating a fairy cake, I'm not giving it."

Ópalo swallowed hard, turned away and walked toward the tower. Some doves pecked at the ground and others followed him, flying into the air and making urgent noises that seemed designed to send Ópalo back.

Mateo crossed his arms over his chest, observing Ópalo's feathers glaring bright in the sunshine as he moved with avian grace.

Ópalo slowed, stopped and sighed. He turned back and headed for Mateo, his blue eyes glowing as he approached.

"It's not easy for me," Ópalo said, a sad smile on his lips. "I've waited for you forever. After that apple my father gave me as a child, I dreamed of the sweet taste often. My whole life I was told that my bride would be even better than apples. No matter that I never wanted a bride. When you appeared, it seemed better than I could have hoped. Once we lay together…even more beautiful than I had ever imagined. But it's not the same for you, is it?"

Ópalo seemed to soften. He studied Mateo for a long moment before continuing. "Some men come to fairyland and leave claiming it was all a dream," he said, his arms coming up to wrap around Mateo's neck. "But you'll know the truth. As for me, I chose you the moment I saw you standing so lost at the edge of the shore. My heart was gone in that instant. But I won't require you feel the same. I will win you over, *mi pájaro*. You don't know me, but I am very patient. We have two more days to learn about each other—if you return."

"When I return. I'm no one's bride or groom, and I never will be," Mateo said, "but I'm unwilling to deny myself the pleasure of your company and body. If you're still willing to give it without the promises you crave."

"I'll take you as long as you'll let me have

you," Ópalo admitted, though it seemed to cost him something to say it. Mateo felt a little tug in his gut and he wished he could smooth the tension out of Ópalo's feathers and rub it free from his neck, which looked stiff as though he was forcing himself not to slump with disappointment.

"When you return," Ópalo began, his expression lightening as he said the words, "we'll have three more days to learn each other. And then three more, and so on. We'll have much time."

Relaxing, Mateo wrapped his arms around Ópalo's back. He might not yet know what to do about his sisters, or his own strange situation. But he had time to let this settle, to enjoy his embraces with Ópalo. To kiss and be kissed. To be taken.

Raindrops, unexpected as everything else that had happened, began to splat into the dirt all around them, streaking in fat lines down the massive dovecote. Ópalo tilted his head up to the darkening sky, revealing his long, slender throat and the Adam's apple that Mateo had sucked on that morning. A drop of rain hit it.

"An afternoon shower. Nothing more, but we'll be soaked through," Ópalo said, reaching up to wipe the drops from Mateo's face. "Should we run for it?"

Mateo shook his head and leaned forward, drawn by Ópalo's fluttering pulse, eager to lick the rainwater from his skin. The doves lifted their wings to flap playfully in the cool water as the rain started to fall in earnest. By the time Mateo and Ópalo did run back to the castle covered in mud, the storm was over and they laughed.

Chapter Eleven

I N THE CASTLE baths—long winding halls of connected heated pools open to the warm sun and cool rain—Ópalo was relieved to leave behind the serious discussions that made his chest squeeze with tight, helpless panic. Patience was an easy virtue to speak of, but a difficult one to practice when all he truly desired was for Mateo to present his heart for Ópalo to take, as Ópalo had already presented his own.

The water was wonderfully warm after the freezing rain, and the breeze from the open walls brought tingling gooseflesh as they splashed and sputtered, wrestled and dunked each other. Eventually, their play dissolved into kisses and another foray into sucking and rutting that left Ópalo feeling well used.

Relaxed and sated, Ópalo sat up out of the water on the ledge that wound along beside the baths with Mateo standing between his thighs, gazing up at him with wet lashes and dark, smiling eyes.

"Was that satisfactory?" Mateo asked shyly, but with a gleam that made it clear he knew the answer.

Ópalo didn't know how he could doubt it. He'd made a loud enough racket to rouse his cousins to cries of ecstatic empathy. "I think you could do with some practice," he answered.

He carefully combed his fingers through Mateo's wet curls, mesmerized by the difference between them and the feathers that sprouted from his own head. "Perhaps tomorrow you could swallow my cock again and I could determine if you've improved at all."

If there was to be waiting and choosing later, then he could play at that too.

Mateo wrapped his arms around Ópalo's waist, turning his head into Ópalo's fingers with an expression of a bird being scratched at just the right spot. "As you wish. I am at your command."

If only that were true. Ópalo shook away the uncomfortable memory of Mateo's unnerving reluctance to understand their relationship. He focused again on Mateo's hair, which was the color of black honey shining in the fading afternoon light.

"It's like thread. Soft thread, the softest thread imaginable," Ópalo murmured. "But it's slippery and slick when wet." He shuddered, feeling the quills of his feathers lift and shake water free from his own head. "Does it hurt when these strands come out?" he asked, noting a few fallen hairs on Mateo's strong shoulders.

Mateo laughed. "I don't even feel it."

"What if you lost many at once?"

"If someone pulled a handful out, you mean? Yes, that would hurt." He laughed again. It was a sound that Ópalo found strange and yet wanted to get used to. It was so different from the laughter of fae—more the gurgling of a brook than a twittering bird.

Ópalo climbed down into the warm shallow water in front of Mateo, carefully studying the growth of beard on his face. It was amazing, astounding and something he'd never seen on a fairy before. "It grows here as well. Scratchy and rough, not soft as on your head. More like the hair around your prick, but shorter."

"I usually shave every day, otherwise it would grow rather long," Mateo said, getting down into the water, his own fingers coming up to graze Ópalo's cheek. "Yours is quite smooth. No bristly feathers grow in there, I see."

Ópalo sat in the bath and continued to

explore the roughness of Mateo's face. "Do you need to…shave now? Will it hurt you to leave it as it is?"

"A beard is out of fashion where I'm from, but if it pleases you it does me no harm to grow it a bit." Mateo's shoulders lifted and fell, and Ópalo couldn't resist kissing them, licking along the line of the right one, up his neck to his ear. Unable to restrain himself when Mateo gripped him closer, he dug his fingers into Mateo's ribs, licked the shell of his ear and wormed his tongue into the hole.

Mateo laughed loudly, convulsed and shoved Ópalo away, crying out, "Ticklish!" Water splashed around them, and Ópalo went under, the bubbles of his breath surfacing noisily as he broke through, shaking the wet off.

"Just as my sisters' dog shakes himself." Mateo chuckled. "Only with more feathers."

Ópalo let Mateo pull him close again, promising not to stick his tongue into his ear again—at least not until they were both recovered and ready to play again. Then, perhaps he'd be horrible and tie Mateo to his nest and tickle him until he begged for mercy. Mateo, flushed as he was from laughing, seemed like he might enjoy that.

"Tell me about growing up in your world," he said. Because if Mateo needed them to know each other, then know each other they would. Ópalo pulled himself back onto the ledge, the water sluicing down his back, and reached for a towel to wrap around his shoulders. He pulled his knees up to his chest to keep warm and watched Mateo spin in lazy circles in the water, his profile glowing in the setting sun.

"I was happy," Mateo said. "Until I was not. Then I grew mostly happy again." He flashed a grin. "That wasn't a fair answer. It's hard to quantify a whole life in a few sentences."

"You were happy before your mother died, and then you were not happy for a long time, and then you eventually grew happy again."

"Exactly. I suppose you know how that feels having lived through your father's death."

Ópalo shrugged and then was ashamed. He wished he could say that he did understand and they could bond over their shared losses. "My father and I started out close. I was his last born child to his favorite mistress. In the end, by the time he passed away…well, it's a long story of disappointments and misunderstandings."

"I'm sorry to hear that." Mateo looked as if he blamed himself for bringing up something so awkward, but then he pushed the matter further. "What came between you?"

"You."

Mateo blinked in confusion. "Me? But I never even met your father."

"No, of course not. You asked earlier, how it was I could be so sure you're the one for me. The truth is, I wasn't always certain of you, *mi pájaro*. At times growing up, I was quite sure the bride Father and Lámina had arranged for me was little better than a prison."

Mateo's dark eyes sparked with interest, and he drew closer, standing between Ópalo's legs. "So you understand my doubts?"

"I was told to expect *una novia*, yet I had no wish to lay with a woman. As you can imagine, I was furious with my father. But when I confronted him, he told me to be patient, to have faith in Lámina. I cursed him and shunned his presence from that point on. Then he passed away. When I saw you, Mateo, I understood. I should have trusted my father more. The damage it cost our relationship is something I can never take back. Father died while I was still angry with him."

"I'm sorry."

Ópalo decided to get the unpleasant task over with and simply tell him the rest. "As for my mother, she died when I was born. I never knew her. I heard she was a lovely woman. My siblings liked her well enough, though she was not their own mother. Cacatúa took care of me, and all the others helped of course, but it mostly fell to Cacatúa and Canario."

"You didn't have a nurse?"

"No. Fairy children are different from humans, I'm told. Our infancy is short lived and we grow into adulthood much more quickly than our human counterparts. I've been of age for several years now, but you have only just reached full maturity, have you not? That's one reason the wait for you to come seemed so very long to my older siblings."

Mateo seemed to ponder this. "So if my sisters and your brothers were to bring forth children…?"

"They would likely grow up a bit faster than they would in your world, but their humanness would slow their maturity a bit. At least, that is what we've been told. It's been a long time since our kind took brides from your world."

"Has something changed then?"

Ópalo sighed. "Our world needs the stability of human love to hold it. We need the strength of human hearts. After a certain number of years, as the humanness leaves our blood, we are born hungry for it. And often one brave fairy will take up the task of providing brides."

"Lámina."

"Indeed. She was your nurse, was she not?"

"She was. A good one at that."

"I'm glad to hear it."

"She told the best stories." He pushed back slightly and indicated the room with his hand. "It seems they were not so fantastical after all." He grinned. "As a child, did you hear fairy stories?"

Ópalo laughed. "Of course! We never had a nurse, but we had a tutor, and my father was adept at weaving tales. As were my older brothers and sister."

Mateo swam close again, and rested his cheek against Ópalo's thigh, saying drowsily, "My sisters were always far too interested in their own pursuits to spend much time on me and Luz. But as Father says, Luz and I were thick as thieves. We had our secrets we kept from the others. It made us feel important. Father always encouraged our little club. He believed that Luz and I were special, though Adelita has always been his favorite."

"You're close to your father, then?" Ópalo ran his hand through Mateo's wet curls again, letting them twist around each of his fingers.

"Very close." Mateo turned into Ópalo's strokes. "He's always held a bit tightly to us all. He was so full of grief when my mother died. It's part of why…well, I've never felt that love was all that useful. Not when it leaves a person so lost when it goes away."

Ópalo's fingers stilled. "Must it go

away?"

Mateo sighed and swam off, splashing idly at a dry patch along the edge of the bath. "Now you sound like Papá when I've confessed my thoughts to him on the subject." His voice took a bitter turn. "Of course, he's now in the midst of bargaining my hand away, so I have no idea where 'love' is on the agenda for him any longer."

"He's getting older."

"Yes, and he fears he's losing us. Well, losing my sisters, and he's desperate to know where they go and what they do. Desperate to take control again, even if that means marrying us off to someone we don't love and who likely will not love us."

Ópalo cleared his throat. "This king who wants you…he doesn't love you?"

"Oh, he loves me. If what he feels can be called anything at all, I suppose it can be called that." Mateo's mouth twisted in an unpleasant way. "It's hot and passionate, and he wants me to smile all the time. There's no doubt he desires my joy, but I feel nothing for him. I never could."

"Just as you feel nothing for me." Ópalo felt the hole in his heart throb with barren hope as he spoke his fear.

Mateo's head came up. "No. It isn't the same. I…well, I can't give you what you most desire, but I feel…more for you somehow. An affinity. Passion. I definitely feel passion."

Ópalo swallowed, almost afraid to feel relieved, but still taking heart in Mateo's words. "Yes, humans are different creatures. Love is not something that comes so easily to them. At least, not without enchantment."

Mateo frowned and pushed a wet lock out of his eyes. "Let's leave this behind before you grow any sadder. Tell me more about your childhood. Did you and Azulejo have a special bond?"

"Azulejo was my best friend growing up, but even so he and I are quite different. He's insouciant and I'm a bit more serious. At times we complement each other, and at other times we drive each other mad."

"And your other siblings?

"I have never meshed well with Halcón. He's always doubted my paternity for unknown reasons, and there are few good feelings between us. But the rest of my siblings and I get along most of the time."

Mateo hesitated before asking, "And your father? It seems quite sad how things ended between you."

Ópalo pulled the towel around his shoulders tighter. It had been a very long time since he'd allowed himself to use the word sad when it came to his life. Still, it did bring an ache to his throat remembering how much he wished he could see his father's eyes shining at him one last time.

"I do wish I could tell him how sorry I am for wasting our last years together. I've wished that for a long time, even before I saw you by the lakeside."

Mateo's expression softened. "I understand."

"But every life has such difficult disappointments, do they not?"

Mateo's eyes flared with recognition and he nodded. "Indeed."

"Perhaps so, but it isn't an aspect I like to dwell upon."

"Of course."

"I'd rather talk about how good I am at building things," Ópalo said, sitting up taller and thrusting away the painful thoughts. "I'm a wonderful carpenter and celebrated for my work, even if my brothers and sister say I would be better off spending that time socializing with the court or learning more about politics, treaties and vast-but-boring holdings."

"What do you build?" Mateo asked, hefting himself up onto the ledge too. His dark, hairy legs rubbed against Ópalo's in an exciting and new way that made Ópalo's breath catch. Memories of their rutting crashed through his mind—the rough texture of Mateo's legs rubbing against his hips as he thrust into Mateo's clenching heat. He flushed, bit down on his lower lip and looked down at Mateo's prick. Was it still too soon?

"Hello, have I lost you?" Mateo asked, waving a hand in front of Ópalo's face, his cheeks bright with color and his eyes turning rather hot.

"Tables, chairs, birdcages, desks, bookcases, boxes with secret compartments, almost anything you could want that is made by hands skilled with wood."

Mateo's lips quirked up. "Your hands are quite skilled with my wood," he whispered, sounding ashamed of his own joke, but laughing too.

"I could show you other things I'm skilled at. I'm told my tongue has no rival when properly employed," Ópalo murmured, unfolding himself and pushing Mateo onto his back. The hard stone of the ledge under his knees was distracting, but that was forgotten as soon as he thrust Mateo's legs apart, staring down at his thick, hard cock and the tight sac beneath it. He spit on his fingers and rubbed them over the exposed head of Mateo's prick, pleased when Mateo's eyelids fluttered and he bit down on his lush lower lip. "Lift your legs. I think you'll like this, *mi pájaro.*"

Mateo's choked, shocked, high-pitched shout of surprise only encouraged Ópalo when he lunged forward, pushing Mateo's legs up higher, and worked his face between the cheeks of Mateo's ass. As he trilled his tongue over Mateo's tight asshole, feeling the muscle flex and clench against the tip of his tongue, Mateo cried out and kicked, his foot connecting with Ópalo's shoulder hard enough to bruise. Surprised, Ópalo moved back.

Mateo reached down to grab Ópalo by the feathers and urged Ópalo's mouth back into the musky, hot space, whimpering, "Please. More."

Ópalo obliged. He'd practiced this on

many fae, bringing several of them to sweaty, desperate, tear-stained climax. He licked into Mateo's hole, thrusting his tongue inside. Mateo lifted his legs higher, spreading them and opening himself as wide as possible, moaning and gasping.

When Ópalo was sure Mateo was moments away from coming, Mateo suddenly clenched his fingers in Ópalo's hair. Mateo dragged him up, kissing him before rolling him over and impaling himself on Ópalo's prick. He cried out as he rode Ópalo fast and furious, his long neck tossed back, wet hair throwing water droplets everywhere. His ass gripped Ópalo as Mateo gave over completely to his lust.

Ópalo couldn't get his hands everywhere fast enough. He ran his palms over Mateo's hairy thighs, loving the rough scratch, and up over Mateo's tight abdomen to his chest. He tweaked Mateo's sweet, tight nipples and lurched up to lick and bite them, making Mateo squirm, moan and pull too hard on

Ópalo's feathers.

Without warning, Mateo pulled off, pushed Ópalo's legs up and ducked down to mash his own mouth against Ópalo's hole. Ópalo squawked—for there was no other word for the shocked sound that came from his mouth. He arched and writhed as Mateo shamelessly worked in his tongue, such a quick study. Then Mateo pulled back to slide the thick head of his cock around in the spit he'd left on Ópalo's hole.

"Yes, *mi pájaro*, anything. Take anything."

Mateo pressed in a little and then, as if unable to hold back, he pushed harder. He was barely inside when his face crumpled and he cried out. The wet heat of Mateo's climax spurted into Ópalo's hole and dripped down as Mateo collapsed on top of him, panting.

Ópalo pulled Mateo up to kiss his slick lips, savoring the musky taste. He took his own prick in hand and with a few quick jerks found the edge he needed and flew over it—

fluttering, twittering, singing out as his end-song throbbed in his throat and was swallowed by Mateo's open mouth.

Moments passed—drained, trembling moments. Mateo slipped off him, a grin on his face as he dropped back into the water of the baths. He helped Ópalo down again too, rubbing away the slick spendings from their skin.

"Tables and chairs and bookcases?" Mateo murmured.

"Yes. Would you like to see?"

Mateo grabbed him and kissed his neck, startling a laugh from Ópalo that bounced off the high ceiling of the baths. Birds echoed his joyous sound, swooping just outside on the breeze. "I'd love to see."

Ópalo grinned helplessly. "I didn't realize carpentry would stoke your fires so high. Silly me, hoping to win you over with doves when the thought of hewed wood makes you ardent."

"The thought of you and wood seems to

endlessly intrigue me," Mateo said, and he laughed at his innuendo again.

"I think you should see my workshop, then."

"Indeed, I think I should."

ÓPALO COULDN'T HELP but run his hands over his work as he talked about it. He was proud of the smoothness of the wood, the precise fit of the joints and the sturdiness of his creations. He never used fairy magic in his work, preferring the end result that his own steady hands could make. He pointed that out to Mateo.

"Perhaps it's my low origins," he explained. "My mother was a servant, you see. Of course, my brothers sometimes joke that it's my poor breeding leading me to want some sort of occupation beyond the responsibilities of royalty."

He'd never enjoyed being idle, and while he'd had several lovers since he came of age, Ópalo couldn't entertain himself solely with sex, dancing and politics as his siblings did.

"My sisters are the same about my doves," Mateo said, studying an intricate birdhouse Ópalo in which had taken a great deal of pride. The design was spectacular and when he'd gilded it, he had no doubt that a special cousin would honor him by choosing it for a home. "They tease me about getting my hands dirty, but it's still a gentleman's hobby."

Ópalo smiled softly, showing Mateo how the latch worked on a small box. "Here," he whispered and sprung the compartment. Mateo sucked in air and appeared delighted as he examined the small drawer revealed at Ópalo's touch.

"It's…why, I never would have known to look for it, much less found the compartment itself. It's truly handsome work."

"Thank you. I designed it myself. It took

some time to find the right way to disguise the mechanism. I'm quite proud of it, I must admit. Canario requested one almost just like this for his last birthday gift."

"What does he keep in the compartment?" Mateo asked.

Ópalo lifted a brow. "Only Canario would know that, I'm afraid."

Moving on, Mateo knelt to examine some bookcases and Ópalo knelt too, leaning a hand on Mateo's sturdy thigh as if to balance, but truly in order to feel the heat of him under his palm.

"I have a question," Mateo asked, not looking away from the freshly sanded cases. "Why were you born late? The others…they all came as my sisters did in sets of two and three, did they not? What made you different?"

Ópalo reluctantly pulled his hand away from Mateo's warm leg and stood up, a knot of discomfort in his stomach. "I was born to replace a lost twin. Azulejo's twin originally meant for you."

"You aren't my original fairy soul mate?"

There was a twist to Mateo's words, a humor, but Ópalo frowned at the thought. He hated the idea of Mateo having been originally intended for anyone else.

Mateo's smile faded and he stood too. "That frightens you, doesn't it? Why? Do you worry perhaps we aren't star-destined to be betrothed, or that you might have been excluded from Lámina's machinations?"

"It doesn't bear considering. She wouldn't have sent you otherwise."

Mateo crossed his arms over his chest, cocked his head and narrowed his eyes as he examined Ópalo closely. "Lámina gave me the cloak because I asked for her help. I wanted to find out where my sisters were going at night but didn't know how to trick them into showing me. That's the only reason I'm here. She didn't send me."

Ópalo shook his head. He didn't believe that. He couldn't.

"How do you know Lámina?"

"I have only known her through tales told by my father of the fairy who gave up her life here to bring us brides. Even Cacatúa. Father knew from before her birth she would crave a strong woman and not a man. Wives for us all. Except I didn't want a wife." Ópalo watched Mateo's eyes, how they shifted down and the small crease between the brows grew more prominent. "You wouldn't have wanted a wife either. Azulejo's twin was a girl."

"You're saying Azulejo's twin was killed? Because of what I want?"

Ópalo gasped. "Of course not. She caught fever and died, just as her mother did. Don't be absurd." Yet the seed had been planted. The thought was there. No. His father had been obsessed with the completion of his plan—twelve fae for twelve humans— but he was not a cruel man.

"So you were born then."

"Yes. Born to be your bridegroom."

Mateo sighed and rubbed the bridge of

his nose. "Did my sisters ask any of these questions?"

"The fairy cakes," Ópalo said simply. No other explanation was needed, but he added, "Questions fly from the mind. Pleasure and contentment is sought. They didn't think to ask. They're happy. As they should be." *As you ought to be.*

"Luz seems happy. That I've seen with my own eyes. My other sisters are the same?"

"See for yourself. Dinner is soon. We should prepare ourselves and attend. Of course, you shouldn't eat anything, unless you wish to obligate yourself to return."

"Would you like that?" Mateo asked, running a hand through his hair and looking confused, frustrated. Lost.

"It would make it easier." The admission was necessary. "But no. I've met your inquisitive side and though it troubles me, I suppose I couldn't do without it now. If you ever choose to eat, it will fill me with joy. But as it is, I'll take you as you are."

Ópalo was relieved when Mateo seemed satisfied with that, but still Mateo didn't smile as he had earlier.

"I dread seeing them," Mateo said suddenly, and Ópalo understood. He was proud to finally introduce his "bride", but knew his siblings would have plenty to say about it. If not now, then when Mateo returned. The very thought of rowing Mateo back across the lake and watching him walk away took any appetite Ópalo had worked up during their pleasure.

"They've all been where you are now. They'll be happy you're here."

Mateo snorted. "I doubt it."

Ópalo didn't ask why. He knew. The youngest—least and last—was always considered a likely candidate for tattling and ruining the older siblings' fun, as well as often accused of destroying their most prized possessions. Ópalo only hoped he might end up being prized enough by Mateo that none of them need worry at all.

Chapter Twelve

T HE TABLE WAS full of splendid-looking foods, and his sisters sat around it with their lovers at their sides. Mateo walked a step behind Ópalo, keeping his chin up, determined to meet the gaze of everyone present with firm confidence.

"Mateo," Adelita gasped. She sat at the right hand of a yellow-feathered fairy who must be the eldest, Canario.

The other sisters turned to stare at him, color leaving their faces. They all went still, except for Luz who took a sip of wine and leaned back in her chair, cheeks radiant and eyes shining. "Hi, little brother."

The sisters' lovers placed protective arms about their shoulders, challenges in their eyes. The woman with her arm around Herminia sported a terrifying glare of red-fringed feathers. Mateo followed Ópalo wordlessly to the two empty chairs near the foot of the table and sat down at his left.

His sisters remained frozen, eyes wide. Luz took another sip of wine and lifted her glass in the air. "A toast to our brother, the surprise bride." She laughed gaily.

Mateo said nothing. Ópalo's hand on his arm was cool and it calmed his desire to rush in with a display of temper. Instead, he just looked each of his sisters in the eye, staying quiet as Ópalo waved a pretty servant over to remove Mateo's plate and fill his wine glass.

"Mateo will not be supping with us." Ópalo looked pointedly at Canario. "Shall we make introductions, brother?"

His sisters slowly relaxed as their lovers introduced themselves to Mateo and it became clear that he was not going to attempt to take off anyone's head or stir up an ugly cock fight at the dinner table.

"This was your doing, I suppose," Adelita finally said, her voice tight as she glared at Luz.

"Mateo thinks for himself. He discovered where we were going. I simply didn't mention that I thought he was following us. I'm shocked you didn't realize it, Adelita, reeking as he did of cologne. I'm glad you bathed him, Ópalo. He's more endurable now."

"What will you do?" Catalina asked Mateo, her hands twisting together and ignoring her sisters. "When we return, will you turn us over to Papá?"

"Or will you join us in this double life?" asked Blanca, her pale eyes glowing with fire and hope.

Mateo looked at Ópalo's pink feathers and flashing eyes, admiring the fairy power that poured from him. "I'm not a bride, as you have deemed yourselves to be. I've entered into no betrothals and made no promises."

The fae at the table began to vibrate, their feathers puffing and bristling.

"Regardless, I'm not one to deny love where it's bloomed, or to insist promises made in steady affection be tossed aside due to the unexpected nature of the suitors. And I have reasons of my own to agree to your engagements and to want to return to this place myself."

"So you'll keep our secret."

"I didn't say that. You all must know that it cannot be kept. There are men and women in competition for your hands seeking to crack open this mystery. They are going to lengths both extreme and ridiculous. It can't hold."

Adelita and Blanca looked at each other, and then nodded. Mateo met each of his sisters' eyes and said, "We require a plan."

"Then you're an ally." Adelita spoke for all of them as usual.

"Have I ever been against you?"

"Yes," Gracia declared. "There was the time you wanted our little Whitey banished for chasing your doves."

"In anything that mattered?"

"Whitey matters."

"*¡Dios mío!* Gracia, I'm talking about your marriages and a way to legitimize them in Papá's eyes and you wish to argue about your dog?"

Adelita laughed softly and agreed. She lifted a glass of wine to Mateo and took a sip, her cheeks glowing and her eyes growing hot. The temptation to steal a bite of the fairy food beckoned to him, but he fought it off.

"I dare say, little brother, with you on our side, we may have found a way to have what we all want. Papá will never deny you, his very favorite child."

Mateo couldn't stop himself from scoffing. "Has the fairy wine muddled your head? You know full well that you have always been Papá's favorite, Adelita."

"Don't be dim, Mateo. You are his only son and you only look at something and he provides it for you. That damn dovecote for one!"

"Oh please, yes, let's have this fight," Luz said, her words rich with the effects of the wine. "Everyone here wishes to know who's Papá's true favorite."

A scattered response of "Adelita" and "Mateo" came from the other sisters.

"Perhaps your father has two favorites," Canario said, resting his hand on the back of Adelita's chair. "That cannot be so unusual."

"Who was your father's favorite, Canario?" Elisa asked, her fork poised to stab into another piece of cake.

"I was, of course."

No one disputed him.

"It is decided then," he went on, clapping his hands together with authority. "Mateo will speak to your father and soon we will all be wed. This is cause for celebration! But first, finish your meals." Canario's yellow feathers fluffed beautifully in the candlelight. "There is dancing to be had!"

Ópalo, who had been looking vaguely worried ever since Mateo had denied being betrothed to him, suddenly smiled and leaned forward, clearing his throat to get everyone's attention. He nodded toward Mateo. "He is really a lovely bride, isn't he?"

As Mateo swallowed down his irritation at being called a bride, his sisters choked and laughed, and Imelda went so far as to voice her agreement with jeers and entirely inappropriate hand gestures. Mateo wondered how she had turned out so very crass, but noticed Gallo truly didn't seem to mind, and even shared her penchant for crudity.

"I see you've stopped shaving, brother," Blanca said once she caught her breath.

"Such a manly bride," Luz said, laughing. "He is divine, Ópalo, truly."

"I agree," Ópalo said, giving Mateo a long look that left nothing to the imagination.

Mateo felt warm and stopped himself from biting into his lower lip. The last thing he wanted was to give away to his sisters how thoroughly aroused Ópalo left him. Adelita was finally treating him like someone with something to offer and while they no doubt knew exactly how he was spending his time with Ópalo, he didn't wish to give them anything more to tease him about.

Not until he'd convinced his father to legitimize his sisters' commitments to their fae, anyway. Then they'd all owe him an immense debt of gratitude that no amount of teasing could overcome.

AFTER ANOTHER NIGHT of dancing and his third day in fairyland spent alternately trysting and exploring the various halls and rooms of the castle—and then trysting in them too—Mateo was exhausted. He didn't think he had the energy for another evening of revelry, but Ópalo insisted they not miss out.

"Have you noticed you're not aching?" Ópalo asked, swiping a finger against Mateo's well-used asshole when Mateo bent over to pull up his new trousers. They were made of pink feathers mixed with dove down. Mateo suspected the pink was Ópalo's, though he didn't ask.

"Let me guess, your fairy seed magically heals me."

Ópalo laughed, his cheeks turning red. "No, of course not. It's the healing water of the baths." His feathers fluffed in amusement.

Mateo blinked. "Because magical healing water is much more reasonable than magical healing seed?"

"Of course!"

Mateo laughed and kissed him.

Looking pleased, Ópalo said, "And it's

not just the baths. All the water of my land is healing. It helps prevent disease, which leads to our longer lives. It heals wounds. Even the most deadly if the water is applied soon enough and in sufficient quantity."

Mateo chuckled. "Then how does one of your kind ever die? Why are you not immortal?"

"There are a few sicknesses the water is powerless against, and there are some wounds too mortal for it to cure. And in the end, we all must pass on to the next world. In humans, it's less effective against aging and illness, but it heals most wounds quite easily, and can slow down the aging process so you become suitable mates and companions for us."

Mateo pondered this as he continued dressing. While most of the day had been spent pursuing pleasure, he'd spent an hour that morning with his sisters discussing how to break the news of fairyland and the sisters' engagements to their father.

Although Mateo could see in Adelita's imperious gaze that she thought herself in charge, he didn't entirely approve of her plan. It was simply to continue as they were, allowing chancers to attempt to discover their secret until they were forced to reveal themselves.

"He is old, Mateo," she'd said. "There may be no need to tell him at all."

"You would rather he die despairing of his daughters than to brave the truth with him?"

"What if he isn't pleased?" Catalina whispered, her eyes brimming with tears.

"How could he be more displeased than he is now? At least he'll have answers."

They'd agreed to go with Adelita's plan for several more nights, but Mateo wasn't sure he had it in him. If he had to endure the longing stares of King Hernando for even one more day, he wasn't sure he wouldn't blurt out the truth over dinner, and his father deserved privacy for this revelation.

"Mateo," Ópalo asked from the doorway. "Are you ready?"

Mateo adjusted his new clothes, enjoying the play of the feathers in the light. His light beard made him look less baby faced. Older and somehow stronger. He thought he was rather handsome, if he did say so himself.

"Does the water work outside of your world?" Mateo asked thoughtfully, thinking of his father's gray hair.

Ópalo crossed to him, ran a hand down Mateo's chest and gazed up at him earnestly. "Yes, but it can't reverse time. You're thinking of your father, aren't you?"

"Yes." Mateo fingered Ópalo's soft feathers. "May I take some with me when I go?"

"Of course."

Nuzzling Ópalo, Mateo scraped his cheek along Ópalo's neck, earning him a gasp and a kiss. "Let's go," Mateo said. "Before we stay."

The dancing was no less fervent and inspired the third night. Mateo had never imagined he would allow himself to be fucked up against a wall in a crowded ballroom, but everyone was lust drunk, and no human or fairy could spare a moment to look at him, so caught up in their own dancing and desperate lovemaking that he'd become invisible even without the cloak.

The night had worked something wild on him, and he was more aflame with desire than he'd ever known possible. The cacophony of music, birdsong and cries of ecstasy served only to keep him flushed and aroused until he followed Ópalo away from the dance.

On his elbows and knees, Mateo gripped the soft fabrics of Ópalo's nest in his fists, grunting with each rapid thrust of Ópalo's cock. He'd started this encounter with the intention to tumble Ópalo to the bed, open him up and get his own cock into Ópalo's small body, since perhaps that was as it should be. That Mateo should prove his manhood. But between his lust and Ópalo's talents it had not gone to plan.

Ópalo was a distracting and persuasive lover. Not with his words, but with his tongue and his fingers. The next thing Mateo knew, he was rubbing his face in the pillows while Ópalo buggered him, sharp chin digging into Mateo's spine and his arms wrapped around Mateo's middle, holding on tight as they moved together.

Mateo had to admit that in his heart of hearts, this was how he longed it to be—his secret, deepest desires made real. On his knees, submitting to his lover, being filled with cock. Being completed.

It was only the third day Mateo had known what it was to be taken in this way, and he was getting to be good at it, he could tell. Mateo worked his hole to milk Ópalo of more pleasure as he gripped on Ópalo's slow pull out.

"That's it. That's so good, *mi pájaro*. Delicious. Tight."

Filthy, slick noises squelched between

them, and Mateo smelled the musk of their earlier sex all over the pillows he rubbed against his face. He breathed deeply, fire burning in his veins.

"Squeeze me. Yes, tighter," Ópalo gasped. "So good, my bird."

The intense drag of Ópalo's cock and Ópalo's mutterings spiraled through Mateo, leaving him racked with need. He let go of the sheets, wormed a hand down to grab his own hard cock, and moaned. Unbearably sensitive, his prick was so hot and hard and throbbed with such desperate urgency that his hand didn't feel like enough. He gripped it ruthlessly, pressing the tip of his thumbnail just under the head so that the pain dulled his frantic need. He whined and bucked into Ópalo's strokes.

"Shh," Ópalo hushed him, pulling Mateo's hand away and replacing it with his own. "Let me have you."

Mateo buried his head in the nest again, letting his hips go, rutting forward into

Ópalo's hand and then back onto his prick, moaning and sweating, tossing aside everything but his insistent craving for release.

"Harder! Harder!" he cried.

Ópalo gave him what he needed. His hand jerked fast and urgently, his hips snapped forward with loud, smacking thrusts, and Mateo's mind was ablaze. His balls curled with heat before he convulsed, waves of pleasure shattering over him. He smelled his own spendings first, before the shock of the climax hit him fully. His stunned cry burned his throat, until the full height and depth of his pleasure shuddered through him and he was sure he'd never recover from the grandeur of it.

Still shuddering, he dropped into the nest, rubbing his cock against the soft, seed-spattered blankets. Mateo trembled through another wave of pleasure, his limbs jerking and twitching while Ópalo moved slowly still inside him.

"That was beautiful," Ópalo whispered, pushing sweaty hair from the side of Mateo's face and never letting up his strokes.

Mateo was too tired to squeeze any longer and he felt Ópalo move more easily in and out. He let himself relax into the rhythm, taking the thrusts limply, whimpering when Ópalo slammed over the place inside that seemed to blind his eyes with sunlight even in the dark of night. Gradually Ópalo increased the pace, clearly seeking his own climax. Mateo spread his legs, opening himself as much as possible, wanting more of Ópalo's thrusts, eager to feel his prick pulse inside him and fill him up.

"You…" Ópalo hitched Mateo's hips up, and he followed the motion, clambering to his hands and knees gamely, despite his exhaustion. "There. Just there, *mi pájaro*. Take it, take me. Yes."

Then Ópalo was throbbing, singing, pulsing, shuddering all over as he reached his pleasure and Mateo felt the hot, slick seed pushing out around Ópalo's still thrusting cock to slip down over his balls in a wet, warm rush.

After, they lay in a heap together, sweaty and naked. "Tomorrow you leave," Ópalo said. "You'll be gone for three days, and my heart will ache, I'll miss you so."

Mateo kissed Ópalo's feathers, tucking Ópalo's head under his chin. He didn't know how to respond. He knew that the coupling they engaged in was intense and so powerful that he didn't want to even imagine going back to a life without it. But perhaps pleasure with another was always like this?

He'd never lain with any of the courtiers. Would it be the same with them? No, he didn't think it could be. He could think of no one, other than Sir Franco, he might want to lie with—and even the knight seemed boring and staid in comparison to Ópalo with his brilliant pink feathers, beautiful carpentry and fanciful birdhouses. His fairyland.

Still, Mateo couldn't say if his heart was fully aligned with Ópalo's just yet. He still barely knew him. He was definitely dazzled, of that he had no doubt.

One thing was for certain. Being with Ópalo had cemented that he would never be strong-armed into marriage to King Hernando or anyone else who didn't inspire as much lust and desire as Mateo felt even now tangled in Ópalo's bed, with damp, pink feathers sticking to their arms and legs, a tide of exhaustion washing over him.

It simply could not be.

Chapter Thirteen

MATEO SAT SULKING—THERE was no other word for it—upon his high-backed chair next to his father's throne as the ministers talked endlessly of finances and alliances. He twisted his head from side to side and rolled his shoulders, restless and eager for the council meeting to be over so he could speak to his father alone.

He was even more eager for night to fall so he could return to Ópalo. It was astonishing that time could drag in such a way that the mere hours he'd spent away from fairyland felt twice as long as the days he'd spent wrapped up in its birdsong.

His eyes were drawn to the gray stone ceiling, a marvel of human innovation when the castle had been constructed, or so his tutors had instructed him. But it was nothing compared to the open wonder of Ópalo's castle. He shivered, remembering the baths, a serpent of warm delight winding through to many secret alcoves, giving privacy to consummate one's affection in wet bliss. There was always time for bliss in fairyland.

"Now we must return to the pressing matter of the princesses."

Mateo sat up straighter at that, his mind dragging away from the memory of Ópalo fluttering his feathery eyelashes against the head of Mateo's cock, leading Mateo to beg for his tongue, his lips, his mouth, anything—just more.

"Indeed," his father said, rubbing a hand over his eyes wearily. "Hernando failed last night, but he intends to try again."

"God save us all," someone muttered and the king nodded.

"That infernal bell. Perhaps tonight he will be successful, lest we lose two more nights of rest to this madness." His father sighed miserably. "Let us not discuss it further now. What is there to say?"

The courtiers left the room at his father's hand wave of dismissal and Mateo couldn't fail to notice how slowly his father moved as he stepped down from the dais.

"I missed you at breakfast, Papá," Mateo said, walking beside his father as they started down the long corridor leading to his father's chambers. Mateo found all of the rooms rather grim and dark now. It had always been home, but now that he saw it with freshly scrubbed eyes, it was hardly a cheerful place. "I was left alone with only my sisters to ward off the ugly advances of King Hernando."

His father groaned. Mateo half expected a lecture on the suitability of Hernando and Mateo not turning into an ingrate like his sisters. Instead his father rubbed a tired hand over his face again and muttered, "He truly is an imbecile. I regret throwing you into this, Mateo. You should not pay the price for your sisters' lies."

Mateo sensed an opportunity. "Then we can call off the whole endeavor?"

"Alas, no. We must finish what we've begun. I'm sorry, Mateo, but my honor is too compromised as it is. I can't afford to appear weak or indecisive. With any luck, the man will fail again. If he doesn't? Well, he is taken with you and will likely allow you other lovers. It is a workable arrangement."

Mateo's gorge rose. "I don't find it workable at all, Papá."

"No, I suppose not." He sounded so weary and his skin was so gray that Mateo feared he might collapse at any moment. He guided him to the bed. "Sit. Rest. It's been a long night."

Mateo settled his father and pondered what to say. He smoothed his hand over his freshly shaven cheek. He'd begun to enjoy being unshaven. It had felt strangely freeing.

Sitting beside his father, he took his hand. In the darkness of his father's chamber, Ópalo seemed unreal, as if he was only a dream. Mateo almost wished the waters of fairyland hadn't worked so well—at least then he'd still feel the effect of their times together.

He sighed, thinking of his sisters and their lovers, of Ópalo and all they were hiding from their father. He was an accomplice to it now. But his father was so weakened. Could his old heart bear the truth? What of Mateo's own heart? Parting from Ópalo had been harder than he imagined.

THE SUN AT the side of the lake shimmered against the diamond woods, sending rainbow light everywhere. It danced over Ópalo's skin, coloring him as brightly as the birds he claimed as cousins.

"I'll return tonight," Mateo said, touching Ópalo's smooth cheek.

Out of the corner of his eye, he could see his sisters bidding goodbye to their lovers in varying degrees of amorous abandon. He rubbed his thumb over Ópalo's cheekbone, and slipped his hand back to grip the base of his feathered head.

"You'll return in three days," Ópalo corrected, and Mateo nodded. Ópalo handed him a small wooden box. "A gift."

"I have nothing for you."

"Bring me something when you return. An apple perhaps?"

"Of course." Mateo smiled, looking over the beautiful craftsmanship before spying the mechanism. He touched it, springing open the hidden compartment to find a small stoppered bottle. "What's this?"

"The healing waters you requested. Not only might it help your father, but it's my insurance that you, and your sisters, will stay well enough to return to me. Only a few drops do wonders."

Mateo bent forward and kissed Ópalo, his lips firm and soft against his own. He pulled away enough to press his forehead on Ópalo's, gazing down into his eyes. "Why is it so hard for me to go? For me it will only be a few hours before I return."

"I wish I could claim it was love that held you, but my heart tells me otherwise." Ópalo pressed a hand against his chest.

Mateo kissed him again and forced himself from the boat onto the sparkling crushed-diamond shore. He looked back only once to see Ópalo standing forlorn in his boat, watching Mateo leave.

He followed his sisters through the forest of diamonds, then gold and finally silver. They had donned the clothes they'd arrived in, and after all the walking and the dancing of the first and last nights, his sisters' slippers were in near tatters. His own boots were little worse for wear, though. He carried the cloak in his arms, the need for invisibility past.

Eventually the path through the forest of

silver led them to a shimmering circle of light hanging mid-air. Mateo watched as one by one his sisters stepped through. He was the last—and the sensation was almost like falling. A rush of wind, a shriek of noise and then he stood in the air outside his sisters' window casement, the stars a shining map of magic stretched out above his head.

Luz reached out the window, grabbed his hand and jerked him inside. "Don't stand there gawking, baby brother. If the portal were to close with you not quite through, well, I suppose at best you'd fall to the courtyard below and break your legs, and at worst your neck."

King Hernando was still slumped upon the floor, snoring and drooling.

"Ópalo is a much better looking husband, Mateo," Imelda said. "Surely you would rather have him than that old dog."

Mateo felt sudden heavy exhaustion drop onto him. He hadn't even realized he was tired, but now he could barely stand. All of his sisters seemed to slump at the same moment.

"It's closed," Adelita murmured.

Looking at his sisters' faces, Mateo could see the fairy thrall had broken. Their eyes were tired and duller somehow, although he supposed it was how they'd always looked. Mateo took Adelita by the arm, her smooth skin cool under his hot palm. "Tell me you still love him."

Adelita's smile was small but genuine. "I love him, Mateo."

"And you, Blanca?"

"Yes, it's true. I love him."

Down the line of them Mateo went, and each sister confirmed that even now she loved the fairy she'd left behind with all her heart. He sighed, and they all jumped and shouted when the loud clang of King Hernando's bell filled the room. Hands to their ears, his sisters glared at the drooling, drugged sleeper on their floor.

Mateo nudged King Hernando with his

boot. He moaned Mateo's name softly, much to the sisters' snickering amusement. Mateo rubbed a hand over his hair, exhausted and overwhelmed in an entirely different way than he had been his first night in fairyland. "I bid you all good night. We'll talk more on the morrow."

Luz followed Mateo to the antechamber, closing the room to their sleeping quarters behind her softly. "Mateo, wait."

"Yes?"

"What of you? How do you feel now that the portal has closed?"

Mateo studied her black eyes, shining up at him and so full of worried love. "I...." He paused, searching himself for emotion, and didn't know if he was surprised to find his affinity for Ópalo didn't seem much lessened. The difficulty of having left him behind was gone, but he still desired to return to him that night and, if given the choice, he'd be happy to find Ópalo in his bed when he reached his chambers. "I feel tired," Mateo finally said.

"But about Ópalo?"

"It's a complicated emotion." Only it was not complicated at all. He liked Ópalo, enjoyed his company, thoroughly loved the intimacies they indulged in and felt a warm affection he had not felt for anyone else before. But it still did not match with Ópalo's expectations, or mirror Ópalo's feelings for him.

Luz's brow furrowed and Mateo smoothed it with his fingers. "Shh, Luz. I need some rest. Come now, help me leave." He kissed her forehead and swung the cloak over his shoulders. He slipped out the main door, Luz's voice ringing right behind him as he skimmed past the guards, who all lurched into position to block the sisters from attempting an exit.

"I'm hungry," Luz said. "Please call for a small loaf of bread."

Mateo then turned the corner of the hallway leading to his room, but he didn't remove the cloak until he was safely inside his quarters with his back against the door, his chest heaving with strange emotions that he was simply too tired to attempt to understand.

EVEN NOW HE was confused by his feelings for Ópalo, and though he should be concentrating on what to do about his sisters' engagements and on how to reveal the truth to his father, he had to admit that whenever he let his thoughts stray away from sex with Ópalo and more toward Ópalo himself, the unwanted stirring of his heart confounded and concerned him.

"What troubles you, Mateo? Aside from your heartless sisters, I mean?"

Mateo smiled and kissed his father's knuckles before answering the question. "Father, when did you know you loved our mother?"

A soft smile spread over his father's face and though his eyes remained closed, Mateo thought he was seeing something wonderful. "Ah, your mother. Well, I was slow to believe, you see. My old nurse told me when I was about your age that I should marry your mother, but I insisted I was far too well positioned to marry a princess from a lower station than mine." He laughed a little. "The arrogance of youth! But then it seemed another would have her hand, and I realized my feelings were such that I was going to kill the man if she accepted him. Oh how my old nurse laughed at me then!"

"Was she like Lámina?"

"My nurse? Heavens no. She was no mad fairy like old Lámina."

Mateo startled so that his father opened his eyes. "You know?"

"What, my boy?"

"That Lámina is a fairy?"

His father chuckled. "Of course I'm

aware of her yarns. Old Lámina came to us years ago, a mad little lady, spinning a tale of fairyland. She told us she'd given up her youth, her life and her kingdom to come be the nurse to our children. Your mother found her delightful, and I could never refuse your mother, so I agreed. I've often laughed at her story, but she has always been dedicated and wise when it comes to the twelve of you."

Mateo whispered. "Have you spoken to Lámina about where she thinks our sisters go at night?"

His father pulled his hand from Mateo and waved it beside his own head. "She thinks they go to fairyland. I cannot tell if she is laughing at me or if her mind has truly gone."

Mateo nodded slowly. "I see."

"Leave me now. I need sleep so that I can help King Hernando tonight with his new plan." He groaned again. "How he slept through that infernal bell when it kept the rest of the castle awake, I'll never know."

Mateo brushed his father's hair back from his face, watching his tired eyes close. He kept up the gentle caress, remembering how Lámina had stroked his forehead in just this way as a child until he'd drifted off into dreams. His father's hair was fine under his fingers, white and steel-gray mixed. Truly, what was he waiting for? His father deserved to know.

"Father, I know how he slept through it."

"Good, good," his father's voice sounded half asleep. "Perhaps you can help him stay awake tonight."

Mateo stood, reached into his pocket and pulled out the silver leaf, the gold leaf and the diamond leaf. When he had them in his hand, he said, "Look, Father."

But the moment had passed.

Mateo watched as his father began to snore softly. The leaves glittered in his hand, and he set them on his father's bedside table. He flicked his eyes over the room he'd always loved so dearly—the soft couches and tables, the wardrobe that still held his mother's carefully preserved dresses. It was just as it had always been, but he wanted to throw the windows open, let in the light.

He strode to the closest window and unlatched the shutter. He gazed down at the tossing sea that churned on the soft sand shore. It was gray and white, tired and old, like his father. How had his view of his world been so changed in the span of one human night? His eyes strayed to the small house near the herb gardens. Leaving the shutters unlatched and the leaves he'd gathered in the fairy forest on the table, he left his father to rest.

Lámina smiled at his approach, her teeth the same stained brown they had always been. The herb garden was still lush, but somehow less green and verdant after the dazzling world of the fae. "You return!"

Mateo held the cloak out to her.

"No, no, it is a gift for you." She waved

it off, but eventually took it from him when he didn't drop his arms. She put it aside on a bench and took hold of his hands, examining him closely.

"So, my favorite boy, you went. Old Lámina sees that clearly. But you didn't eat?" She clucked her tongue. "The doves had told me the youngest fairy was unpredictable and yet moral. I should have guessed. What is his name?"

"Ópalo," Mateo said.

"Yes, now I recall. Ópalo. We fae do enjoy colorful names." She took his arm and they strolled toward the house together, the scent of mint rising around them as they walked. "If this young prince, Ópalo, told you not to partake, he is a brave one indeed. Few fae would risk a human's own judgment. They are too desperate to feed on the love of a human heart. But this is better than I hoped. He will be perfect for you, Mateo."

"Will he?"

"Why he would not be?"

"Because he's a fairy and lives in another land? Because if I do not wish Hernando to be thrust upon me, why would I prefer another admittedly more attractive man who seems to love me even more blindly?"

Lámina smiled. "Because you do."

Mateo rolled his eyes and followed Lámina into her house. The strong, familiar odors were welcoming, and he took a deep breath. The house seemed dark, as all the buildings did to him now. "Do you really prefer the windows closed?" he asked, going to one to open it, surprised to see the latch had rusted, it was so rarely used.

"I like the cold, damp, ugly human world. It sings to me," Lámina said.

Mateo took in her tiny form and tried to decide if she was joking. He thought she was not, and he didn't understand. "Why would you trade there for here?"

"There it is all pleasure, all fun and dancing, delicious things to eat and so little work. I prefer a hard grind to life and the grim specter of men dying young. It adds a certain spice to life that I missed there." She smiled. "I am odd that way, so they say." Lámina tutted at him. "Do not pretend you don't understand me, *mi pájaro*." The endearment sounded wrong coming from Lámina now. Somehow Ópalo had claimed it during the time Mateo had been in his arms.

Lámina studied him. "It is why you hesitate when your sisters flew so willingly away. There is part of you that likes the hardness of this life too."

"My mother was here," he said.

Lámina nodded. "Your lover is there. So you will straddle, as I knew you would. The moment I saw your wrinkled, red face screaming on your mother's tit, I knew you. Still, you will love the fae and the fae will love you. That is how it is. That is how it will always be."

Mateo sat down at her table. He picked up various bunches of herbs and smelled them, until Lámina snatched one from his hand, sniffed at it, chewed a leaf and nodded. "There, give that to your father. It will calm him enough to survive the shock."

Mateo stared at her. "How did you know?"

"Old Lámina knows you, and now she knows of the brave Ópalo. You won't gallivant in secret. You won't keep it from your father. You won't keep it from anyone."

"But what if I never love him?"

Lámina waved the question away. "What if the sun does not rise? What if birds do not fly? What if you never return to the man who makes your blood sing? What if, Mateo?"

"What if?" he repeated.

"Yes, what if?"

The sun was lower in the sky when he left Lámina's house, and he felt a burst of excitement and relief. Shortly he could be with Ópalo again. He thought of Ópalo's fingers in him, the twist of his wrist, the pleasure of him rubbing against the place inside that made Mateo sweat and plead.

Then he glanced down at the bunch of herbs in his hand. His heart pounded for a different reason now. His father—he must tell his father, but—perhaps not tonight? He could have three more days of undisturbed bliss with Ópalo.

"Prince Mateo!"

King Hernando stood on a stone balcony jutting off the side of the chambers he had taken over for the duration of his stay. "Prince Mateo, do come to my rooms. I have a splendid surprise for you!"

Mateo waved at him, but pretended not to understand.

No—he must tell his father tonight. It was time to put an end to this horrible challenge for his or his sisters' hands, and to give his father the truth he deserved. At least with Lámina's odd honesty through the years, perhaps his father wouldn't find the existence of fairyland to have been wholly without warning?

Besides, even one more day of Hernando

and his wooing was entirely too much.

He reached the main castle entrance and had only just bent down to pet Whitey, who leapt and barked for attention, when Luz came running toward him, her skirts nearly making her trip in haste.

"Mateo, Mateo, it's Papá!"

Her hands were like ice when she grabbed hold of his and tugged. Her face was so white, her black eyes stood out like dark stars. "Hurry, the physician sent me to find you!"

"Fetch Lámina," Mateo barked to one of the guards standing watch. "What's happened?" Mateo asked as he and Luz ran together toward their father's chambers. "When I left him a few hours ago, he was sleeping soundly."

"He rose and collapsed in the kitchen while sneaking an early bit of dinner. The younger cooks were in a panic but at least the chef kept a cool head. The doctor was fetched at once and Sir Franco carried him to his rooms."

Outside their father's door, Luz grabbed him tightly. "Wait. Wait, Mateo. They found these by him." She held out the leaves. "Has he collapsed from nerves? Did you tell him?"

"No. Not yet."

She swallowed hard, her eyes on the leaves glittering in her hand. "We should never have lied to him. We've weakened his heart with even more grief. Perhaps he could have borne the truth better after all."

"Shh, don't talk as though he's gone."

Luz's throat worked and tears filled her eyes, spilling down her cheeks. "I wanted him to meet Azulejo, Mateo. I wanted him to see our new home, and to give his blessing. I wanted that so much and now, what if he's left us?"

"He hasn't."

Mateo hugged her tightly, kissed the top of her head and then let her go. Luz's mention of Azulejo had reminded him of something very important. He pushed Luz away and raced back down the hallway.

"Mateo, where are you going?" Luz chased after him. "Papá needs us!"

Mateo ignored her, running to his chambers to fetch the box Ópalo had given him. He triggered the mechanism while Luz watched from his elbow and lifted the stoppered bottle out. "Fairy water," he murmured and her eyes went wide in understanding.

"I have some too," she said. "In my room. Azulejo gave it to me."

"Get it," Mateo said. "Ask the others if they have any as well."

Moments later, they pushed into their father's room. The courtiers moved aside until Mateo was close enough to see and then moved back in behind him. The physician rubbed ointment into his father's chest and the priests said prayers by his head. Mateo was relieved to see his father's chest rise and fall though it was far too shallow for his liking.

"Papá." Adelita's voice was tight from the doorway, and the sea of courtiers parted again to let her through. She took hold of their father's hand and knelt by his side, kissing his knuckles fervently. "He will be well soon?" she asked the physician who simply shook his head.

"Yes." Lámina's voice came over the crowd, and then she was there too, tiny but fierce, with a pot of foul-smelling herbs mashed into a paste. "He will be well."

The physician threw up his hands and rolled his eyes to the ceiling, but moved aside to allow Lámina room to work.

Mateo and Luz shoved their bottles into Lámina's hands. She looked at them and nodded, holding the king's nose pinched between two fingers and then pouring the contents of Luz's bottle and most of the contents of Mateo's down their father's throat.

He coughed and sputtered, but his breathing improved immediately.

Soon the other sisters crowded in, clutching their own bottles of fairy water—all of which were waved away by Lámina. When the room grew too crowded, the physician banished all but family, Lámina and Sir Franco, who stood crammed into a corner, strong arms crossed and a deep, handsome crease of worry between his eyes.

"Thank you," Mateo said softly, drawing close to him.

"I am always honored to serve my king," Sir Franco said, not taking his gaze from Mateo's father.

"I understand, but my gratitude remains. Though he grows old, he isn't light. I imagine he was quite a load to heft despite his poor health."

"I've carried heavier, my prince."

Mateo had seen the knights practice, had arranged his schedule in order to witness their sweaty exertions at times, and he knew Sir Franco spoke the truth. Still, he wanted to ensure that Sir Franco understood his actions would not be unrewarded. "There will be favor shown for your help, good sir."

Franco pulled his eyes away from the king and studied Mateo. "You look quite changed, sir. Are you well?"

Mateo's heart skipped a beat. Could Franco tell somehow? Did Mateo truly appear different? "Aside from worry for my father, Sir Franco, I am well, yes."

"Of course." But Sir Franco uncharacteristically went on, indicating Mateo's face with a sweep of strong, long fingers. "You seem matured, somehow. It suits you."

Luz tugged on his shirt sleeve and Mateo took his leave of Sir Franco, following her across the crowded room to a private corner.

"Mateo, how can you be flirting at a time such as this?" Luz whispered, her wet eyes going from where Lámina still worked on their father to Mateo. "What of Ópalo? Would you throw him over so easily for Sir Franco's boring face? There's not a feather or a spark of magic to be had in that man."

Mateo didn't know where to begin with such accusations. "I was not flirting," he said softly. The words felt trivial in the face of their father's pale, shirtless form still being worked over so urgently by Lámina's rough, old hands. "I feel nothing for him."

"Good."

"But if I did, it would be none of your business, my sister. Nor Ópalo's for that matter. I owe him nothing."

Luz glared at him.

"What?" Mateo demanded.

"Shh!" Adelita looked at them both over her shoulder. "If you are to act like children, get out," she said, nails in her tone.

Luz wiped at her eyes and spun on her heel, leaving the room. Mateo was torn between following to comfort her and staying to watch over his father. In the end, he stayed, and Luz crept back into the room a few minutes later with red-rimmed eyes and shaking hands.

"I just hope the fairy water is enough,"

she whispered. "I thought it would work faster than this."

"He's old. The magic doesn't know what to heal first," Mateo whispered, hoping that what he said was true. "But it will heal him. Eventually."

As the physician despaired, they watched their father fight for his life under the skilled hands of Lámina. Mateo cradled Luz close, tucking her head under his chin. There they all stayed, in clumps of two and three, huddled together.

Chapter Fourteen

Ó pALO STOOD IN his boat waiting alongside his brothers and sister. It had been a long three days, during which he'd made several birdhouses of increasingly elaborate design to give Mateo upon his return.

"They're late." Canario's voice was tight and Ópalo felt more than saw all eleven heads of siblings look to him. "Hours late."

He closed his eyes and listened to the soft splish-splash of the water lapping at the side of the boat. The flowers he'd chosen were all roses, red to bring out Mateo's dark beauty, and pink to serve his own cheeks in good stead as they moved across the lake. He had spent long hours that day thinking of the slow, drawn-out torture that rowing would be. He'd even wondered if they might pause somewhere in the middle and carefully take their pleasure in the bottom of the boat, throwing the flowers overboard for more room, stowing the oars and then rocking together under the moonlight, feeling the gentle roll of the lake beneath them.

"They don't come," Halcón said, his tone vicious.

Ópalo felt it as a slash.

"You should have bade him eat." Cacatúa, who had always stood up for him, seemed ready to cast her lot with the others. Her red feathers crackled with fear.

Ópalo bowed his head. He couldn't deny that the brides were late. He couldn't even claim that he was not wondering at himself— why had he not placed just a little fairy crumb between Mateo's lips as he slept? Yet he still believed with a burning, baseless certainty that Mateo would come.

"Did he promise to return?" Tulipan asked.

Of course Mateo had not promised. He'd said that he wanted to. He'd been reluctant to go, and they'd held hands, they'd kissed, they'd fucked prettily one last time. But no, Mateo had not promised to return.

"Perhaps there's a problem," Azulejo began.

"Yes, the problem is that Ópalo was a fool," Halcón growled.

There was a flash of light and color in the forest of diamonds, and Ópalo's knees went weak. A dove appeared, reflecting rainbows from the trees, and flew directly to Ópalo, lighting upon his outstretched arm. She lifted her foot daintily and cooed.

"Pura," Ópalo whispered.

"What an odd cousin," Cacatúa exclaimed. "She doesn't speak in any language I can understand."

"She comes from their world," Ópalo

said. "She brings a message from Mateo."

A leather strap held the tiny tube, and Ópalo's fingers shook so badly that it was hard to work it free. Finally, he tapped out and unrolled the small piece of paper, squinting to read the few words printed there.

Our father has fallen ill. We cannot come this night. We send our regrets.

"Thank you," Ópalo whispered to Pura dully.

She rubbed her head against his cheek and then flew again, a white-and-gray streak heading back the way she came.

Canario climbed from his boat, shored it up and splashed through the shallows until he reached Ópalo. He snatched up the note and read it before shoving it into the small pocket at the breast of his shirt.

"They do not come tonight," he called to the rest of them. "Their father is ill."

A murmur and twitter went through the others, and Ópalo swallowed hard, looking at his feet, waiting for what he knew would come next. The suspicion had already been raised and now would come the doubts and recrimination. He was familiar with how his siblings' minds worked.

"How can we trust a note from him?" Halcón spoke the question haunting all of their thoughts.

"Luz trusts him," Azulejo piped up, giving Ópalo an encouraging look. "I trust my bride. Do you not trust yours, Halcón? Catalina is fond of Mateo, is she not?"

"Yes, but Catalina is an innocent. I am not so easily fooled." Halcón sneered in Ópalo's general direction. "His lover has betrayed our brides and is keeping them from returning to us."

"Let's not jump to conclusions!" Cacatúa sighed heavily. "The bird was sent to us. That is an act of good faith, I'd say."

"If their father is ill, we must be patient," Canario said, squeezing Ópalo's shoulder, but even his eyes were shadowed with doubt.

"There's nothing for it but to wait until three days hence. Then we'll see if our brides return."

But three days later, their brides did not arrive. Neither did Pura.

"I told you," Halcón thundered. "His lover is keeping them from us. He's probably spirited them away to realms far from the portal, or married them off to hot-blooded humans!"

"What of Lámina? She would send a dove through to tell us if that had happened, would she not?" Cacatúa said uncertainly, looking between Canario and Ópalo as if uncertain who would be best fit to offer her reassurance that her lover was safe and would return to her.

"He's likely killed Lámina," Halcón declared, his claws extended and his feathers rustling with rage.

Ópalo gritted his teeth. "Mateo is no murderer. Their father was ill. They sent a bird last week to tell us. If they do not come today, then it is because their father is worse."

"He gave you no vow." Halcón spit into the water in disgust. "You fool! If you've cost us everything, you misbegotten bastard, I'll show you what pain is." He lunged from his boat, sending it rocking into the waves as he dove for Ópalo's throat.

Canario stepped between them before Halcón could grip anything more than Ópalo's shirt. Canario shoved Halcón away and brought his own claws out in warning. Halcón made as if to attack Ópalo again, but held back when Canario raised his feathers and moved into a fighting stance.

"Our brother is safe until we know more," Canario said. "Do you understand?"

Halcón sneered but nodded, stomping into the waves to capture his boat.

The next three days passed in a precarious and hostile truce during which Ópalo avoided Halcón entirely, and his other siblings as much as possible. He was wretched. His throat was tight and the hole in his heart a freshly carved wound. His mind a tumble of terrible doubt. Had Mateo decided not to return? Was he keeping his sisters from coming back as well? Had he truly been so good at deception?

The evening they were to row out again to wait for their brides, Canario, Cacatúa and Azulejo cornered him in his workshop. He sat at his table staring at the shavings on the floor, unable to work or do more than contemplate in abject misery how the curls of dark wood reminded him of Mateo's hair.

His siblings each pulled up a chair and sat down all around him, their feathers bristling in their obvious discomfort.

Canario began. "Azulejo tells us that you may have more information about this situation than you've shared with us."

"Luz mentioned something odd to me," Azulejo said, looking guilty, but also considerably duller than usual, the anxiety for his bride having cost him feathers and gleam.

"There was a man, a human, who wanted Mateo for himself, was there not?"

Ópalo sat up straighter. "Yes. There was."

Suddenly, his mind was on an entirely different tack than it had been before. Had the man, King Hernando, he believed the name was, discovered Mateo and the others upon their return? Had he presented the information to their father and claimed Mateo for himself, compelling him to honor his father's wishes?

"But Mateo would never agree to marry him," Ópalo said aloud, his heart hammering in his chest and his fingers curling into his palm, claws growing and digging in sharply.

Canario tilted his head curiously. "Marry him?"

"Yes," Ópalo said, hastily explaining the contest attached to their brides' hands.

"You didn't consider this information worth sharing, Ópalo?" Canario asked.

Even Cacatúa looked terrified. "How

could you withhold this from us? We should never have allowed them to return!"

"That is the reason they didn't tell you themselves," Ópalo countered, thumping the table. "They wanted the right to come and go. They're strong-minded women and their love would not withstand being imprisoned here." He saw that his point was nearly made when Cacatúa bent her head and Canario sighed, but Azulejo continued to appear stricken. "You want their hearts, Azul, and if you kill their love by forcing them to stay, their hearts are lost to you."

Canario stroked his eyebrows thoughtfully, smoothing the feathers back and forth. "Did you state that anyone can win one of their hands?"

Ópalo nodded.

"Anyone at all?"

"Yes, assuming the message Mateo sent spoke the truth, and they have not been found out already." Ópalo's eyes caught fire and he sat up even straighter. "I could cross the boundary, tell their father everything and win Mateo for myself."

"At the hazard of your health," Cacatúa reminded him. "Crossing over is dangerous."

Azulejo frowned. "Yes, if you stay too long, you'll become human like them."

"I don't care. Someone must go and retrieve our brides. Everyone agrees that this predicament is likely my fault for failing to feed Mateo cakes and securing his return. Still, I believe he will come when his father is well, that they all will. He knows if his sisters don't return at least once a human moon, they'll suffer greatly. And he loves his sisters. Perhaps Halcón would not believe me, but he truly does."

Cacatúa nodded and took his hand. "I believe you. I saw how he was with Luz and Adelita. He'd not want to watch them suffer. I believe you're probably right, that he does intend to return with them."

Ópalo smiled at her and let her brush her finger through his feathers. "Regardless, if they don't come tonight, I will go to them. You have my word that your brides will return to you."

"And what of you?" Azulejo asked, his blue eyes narrowing.

"I don't know what the human world holds for me or how easy my task will be. But you'll have your brides before their suffering starts, or I'll die trying."

Canario kissed his head and Cacatúa threw her arms around his waist. Ópalo let them hold onto him while Azulejo covered his face with his hands and gave in to soft, sad birdsong.

MATEO MONITORED HIS father's intake of broth, listening to Adelita read from a book from the other side of their father's bed. Mateo was immensely grateful that King Hernando's bell and advances had taken leave of the castle since the contest had been abandoned. He shivered with disgust at the memory of Hernando's wet and inappropriately lingering parting kiss, and swiped at his lips again.

His father grew stronger, and Mateo hoped to tell him the truth soon enough. Hoped his father would accept his sister's fairy grooms. Hoped…for what? His own fairy groom? Aside from his worry for his father, Mateo had been able to think of nothing but Ópalo. He hadn't thought it possible to care for someone so quickly. To miss someone so deeply.

He needed to send Pura through the portal with another note for Ópalo, a note to reassure him that Mateo and his sisters would return. For of course they would. The longing to see Ópalo again—to hold him and touch him and feel the tickle of his feathers on Mateo's skin—was consuming. The men Mateo had once found appealing, like Sir Franco, now seemed drab and ordinary.

Ópalo was so much more. It wasn't just his touch Mateo missed, but the lilt of his laughter, the gleam of his smile. His…everything.

A maid burst in. "Someone has jumped from your sisters' bedroom, my lord! We need the physician!"

"Jumped?" Adelita cried, dropping her book and grabbing her father's hand, wide eyes finding Mateo's. "One of our sisters?"

"A boy. With feathers for hair, or so they are saying in the kitchens. A demon! Or an angel! No one is quite sure."

Adelita gasped, her face going pale. "Feathers for hair?"

"Indeed, my lady."

The king was still frail, but his cool head prevailed. "Adelita, find the physician. Mateo, seek out Lámina. There is probably no hope for the poor boy, but we must do all we can for him. Hurry, children."

Mateo and Adelita didn't need to be told twice.

Chapter Fifteen

MATEO DIDN'T THINK he'd ever seen so much blood.

It was everywhere and coming from various wounds faster than the physician or Lámina could wipe it away. Mateo felt violently ill at the sight of pink feathers soaked black with blood and his lover's broken body smashed on the cobblestone street. Luz's arms around his waist were no comfort.

They'd both run as fast as they could, Mateo stopping only to save Adelita from her skirts twice. The courtyard was crowded with peasants and the courtiers alike, but no one drew too near to the broken body lying twisted on the cobblestones. Birds circled overhead, their cries harsh like screams in the air. Then Mateo saw the feathers that drifted slowly down through the air, landing in the puddles of blood.

Pink.

"No, no," he said under his breath. "No!"

He fell to his knees by Ópalo's head. He put his hands on him, touching him, whispering, "Ópalo, don't. Please don't. Come now. You're all right."

"Mateo," Luz said. "We need the water."

"In my room," he said. "Get the others too."

The rest was a blur of terror. A white-and-red wash of horror consumed him. He saw his sisters crowd around, could hear their voices, and then there was water—not a lot, but maybe enough. Adelita poured what was left of hers over Ópalo's face and Gracia over his chest. One by one they emptied the bottles until Mateo felt the smooth wood of the small wooden box pressed into his hand.

"I don't know how to open it," Luz said softly in his ear.

Mateo thumbed the mechanism and the door sprang open. There wasn't much left in the bottle—less than a third. He'd given most of it to his father. Mateo unstopped the bottle and poured it between Ópalo's bloody lips.

He waited.

There was no change. Mateo's heart hammered so loudly in his ears that he could barely hear the voices of the peasants surrounding them. His sisters sounded as though they were underwater, calling to him from very far downstream. He could only stare at Ópalo's barely moving chest, desperate to hear his birdsong voice.

Then the physician was there shaking his head. "Nothing we can do."

Mateo couldn't process the words in the face of so much blood and the rattle that had started in Ópalo's throat.

Until Lámina shoved the man away, squawking in a sharp tone and moving quickly. Her eyes met Mateo's with a wild urgency and she slapped his cheek hard.

"He needs your help, *mi pájaro!*"

Mateo sucked in a harsh breath and nodded. "What do I do? How can I help him?"

"Give him your heart!"

"What?"

Lámina stared at him, a flash of something horrible in her eyes. She frowned. "You'd sooner see him dead?"

Mateo swallowed hard, looked down at Ópalo's face, swollen almost beyond recognition, and his fingers twitching in spasms that threatened to inch up his arms and take over his whole body. Death throes. The thought of losing him was unbearable. "Yes, yes. Anything!"

Lámina grabbed Mateo's right hand and forced it against Ópalo's chest, then drew up his left to press against his own. "Tell him."

"Ópalo," he said, kneeling low and whispering in his ear. "You can have it. Anything you need. Please don't die…" Mateo licked his lips, trying to find the words. A coldness was starting in his chest, a deep chill that sank into him with a finality that terrified him. "*Mi…mi pájaro*, I'll give you my heart. It's yours. I'll give you anything at all, if you'll only live."

Ópalo's eyes fluttered open, blue and wide, and his mouth twitched into a broken smile. Then he was gone again.

Mateo was pushed aside so several knights could move Ópalo onto a tarp. Putting one foot in front of the other, Mateo followed them to Lámina's cottage, aware of his sisters clotting around him, shifting in and out to kiss and touch him. It soothed through the cloud of numbness and sharp, heightened reality that he didn't quite understand.

When they reached the door to Lámina's

cottage, she shooed the curious peasants and courtiers away. She then grabbed Mateo's chin and gazed up into his eyes. "Do you feel it?"

Mateo stared at her, shaking his head in confusion, his mouth hanging open and his mind awash in terror. "Feel what?"

"His heart, your heart. Do they beat as one?"

Mateo tried to focus on his heartbeat. He looked down at his chest and found it covered with blood, his own hands a mess of red as well. "I feel nothing, Lámina. My heart…feels dead."

A gleam shone in her eyes. "Good." She slammed the door in his face.

WHAT SEEMED LIKE hours passed. Mateo stood there with his sisters, unable to talk, unable to do anything but stare at Lámina's door waiting to know if Ópalo would live. If Lámina could save him. If his heart had been enough.

Finally, when Luz couldn't take it anymore, she pounded on the door and demanded Lámina let them in. "I'll summon the guards to kick the door down, Lámina! Don't think I won't!"

The door opened with a creak moments later, and Luz and Adelita pushed Mateo in first. Their hands felt like ice on his overly hot skin. The interior of the cottage was dark, but the scent of the herbs filled Mateo's lungs and brought him back to himself for the first time since he'd seen the waft of pink feathers in the air around Ópalo's body.

"You wanted in," Lámina croaked by the table where Ópalo was laid out. She stood over him, painting his wounds with a paste the color of algae from the sea. "Come see him. You've already given your heart to him. Don't be stingy with it now, or old Lámina will have something terrible to say about that."

Mateo shuffled toward the table as if his feet were moved by someone else's volition. Ópalo looked as if he was near death. Mateo's heart clenched and he felt gorge rise in his throat.

"The fairy water you and your sisters gave him has healed a few of his wounds, but there wasn't enough. He needs to be doused with it, or dunked even, soaked with the stuff in order to recover fully."

Ópalo's eyes were closed, but his eyebrows and head had been wiped free of blood for the most part. Except he looked different.

"Lámina," Mateo whispered, surprised to find his voice worked after the silence that had seemed to reign over him before. "His feathers are white."

"Indeed," she agreed. "He's changing, becoming human. It's part of the problem. The change is fighting the water's healing. He must go back tomorrow night when the portal opens, lest he change entirely."

Mateo touched the soft feathers, noting that blood still crusted near the quills.

Lámina went on, "Unless that was your plan? For him to join you here in this world?"

"No. No, that was never our plan! No," Mateo whispered. "Why would he come here?"

Lámina lowered her bushy brows at him. "Why? Do not play that game with me, Mateo. You think one note is enough to keep fairies from their brides? Any fool would have known to send a note every night. You're lucky it was just him and not the lot of them lying broken in the courtyard."

"He must have come through the portal and found the window closed to him," Mateo said softly, remembering the lurch of his own heart when he'd found himself walking on air, and the swift jerk of Luz's hand on his wrist pulling him inside.

A collective gasp rose from all eleven of his sisters, crowded around them in the small cottage. They blanched in horror and cried out the names of their lovers as they shoved and pushed their way back out the door, deserting him with Lámina and Ópalo.

"They've gone to open the shutters," Lámina said. "Lest their own lovers come through and meet the same fate."

Mateo nodded. Of course they had. If Ópalo had come through, the others might decide to join him, and then they'd have more dying fae on their hands. Not this one, shuddering soul who seemed so frail, but must be so strong to have survived the fall for even a second.

"He will live?"

Lámina sighed. "Whether as human or fae depends on the timing, but yes, he will live. He will not be undamaged, though. Especially if he becomes human as I did. We simply do not heal as well as the fae." She studied him. "Your heart. How does it feel now?"

Mateo concentrated on his heartbeat, his

throat tight, tears prickling his eyes. There was an ache that seemed all consuming, a gnawing sensation that filled him entirely until he almost couldn't speak the word. "Hurt."

Lámina collapsed into a chair next to the table, set the bowl on the floor beside her and muttered. "Excellent. Now we wait."

Ópalo opened his eyes into a kind of darkness he'd never known. He slowly rolled his head to the side, a horrific pain following the motion. He held in the gasp, uncertain of his safety or surroundings. He appeared to be in some sort of hovel, or a cottage, resting on a waist-high hard surface. Everywhere there were bundles of gray dried vegetation hanging on the walls, and an empty straw-backed rocking chair that was still moving.

Carefully, he rolled his head the other

way and blinked when he saw Mateo sitting with his dark-circled eyes closed, his head leaning back against a wall. There was blood all over his shirt.

Mateo is hurt! The thought jolted him to the core and he sat upright, a wrenching, horrible agony ripping through him. He heard a scream and recognized it was his only after Mateo's eyes flew open. He leapt to his feet, coaxing Ópalo back down again.

"Stop, stop! You have broken bones and myriad other injuries," Mateo said, his voice soft and soothing as a dove's.

"But you're wounded," Ópalo said, his tongue even ached to form words.

"I'm healthy as an ox. It's you who are hurt. Now lie still again."

"The blood." He motioned weakly to Mateo's shirt.

"Your blood, *mi pájaro.*"

Ópalo's eyes flickered. "Why did you call me that?"

"Don't you feel it?" Mateo asked. "I gave

you my heart."

Ópalo frowned and shook his head. "Why? You don't love me."

An old woman with white caterpillar-like eyebrows leaned over the bed. "Hush now. You'll hurt yourself more and you've only just begun to heal. His heart was necessary or you'd have bled out on the pavement. The fools had so little fairy water after giving it all to their father. It's a wonder you survived the fall at all."

"Fall?"

"Careless fairy, popping through a portal without ensuring the other end was a welcoming place to land. It could have just as easily been under the ocean, or in a pit of vipers, but did you think of that? Oh no, you did not."

Ópalo licked his lips, tasting blood on his tongue. "Their room. They said it led to their room."

"Oh, just a few steps shy is all," Lámina said and clicked her tongue. "So I could be sure any visitors from the other side were welcomed guests and not intruders."

Ópalo's body began to shake and his eyes rolled up, and he heard Lámina smack Mateo's arm. "Kiss him. It will help. Have you not heard of the power of love's kiss?"

Mateo dutifully pressed his lips against Ópalo's. Ópalo felt his heart convulse in his chest, a painful flipping feeling that took his breath away. Was this what it felt like to have Mateo's heart? He didn't think so. He felt drained of all that was best in life, tired and on the verge of death.

"There," Lámina said when Mateo pulled away. "Do you feel better?"

Ópalo only murmured, worried his answer would only frighten Mateo and possibly anger Lámina. He was as hollow as ever—hollow and broken. Mateo may have intended to give his heart, but he hadn't. Love, Ópalo understood, couldn't be forced or willed into existence—not in this world. Not without fairy charms. Surely Lámina must have once known that, but perhaps she had forgotten? The fairy waters had done their work to bring him this far from the brink.

"The portal," Ópalo whispered.

"Closed on this end until tomorrow night," Lámina said. "Now tell us, are we to expect more visits from heroic brothers searching for their delayed brides?"

Ópalo whimpered.

Lámina tutted softly. "Let us hope so. It is your best chance."

Unless it is too late. Ópalo could feel the swelling alterations within, making him more human moment by moment. He took a steadying breath and whispered, "How long until the change is complete?"

Lámina bared her crooked teeth in a smile. "It took me three horrible hours, but your injuries are slowing your transformation. Old Lámina is surprised, I must say. Only your feathers have already gone white. At this rate, in several days time they are likely to fall out and you'll grow nice, fuzzy hair like me."

Mateo made an odd sound, and Ópalo glanced his way. "Don't worry, *mi pájaro*. I will get back to fairyland in time. My feathers won't desert me. I promise."

It was an empty vow, but one he made all the same, relieved to see Mateo's expression soften a little.

"Only heal, Ópalo. That is all I ask of you."

"Let the boy sleep then." Lámina waved a strongly scented bottle under his nose.

Then the stars were swimming in Ópalo's head, making rainbows out of blackness.

Chapter Sixteen

MATEO APPROACHED HIS father's room hesitantly. His hair was still wet from the bath he'd taken to wash himself clean of Ópalo's blood. He was almost too tired to be nervous, save for a lingering fear that what he was to reveal would damage his father's health all the more.

He found his father alone, propped in a comfortable chair by his window, pondering something in his hands.

"Papá," Mateo said softly, pulling up a wood chair. He rested his hands on his knees and sighed.

His father held the leaves of gold, silver

and diamond, shifting them back and forth, contemplating them with a serious expression. "I have been expecting you, Mateo," he said. "I believe you have the unfortunate task of telling me the truth, do you not?"

"I do, Papá."

"I imagine you and Adelita tossed a coin for this difficult task and you lost."

"No Papá. Adelita and I are in rare agreement on this front. We both thought I should be the one to talk to you."

"The young man with feathers, the jumper the maid saw. He did not jump, did he?"

"No, Papá."

"These leaves, they are rather remarkable. Are there truly forests of them?"

"Indeed. How did you know?"

"Before you were born, long ago, your mother and I would listen to Lámina telling stories to your older sisters. There was one, a particular favorite of hers, about twelve royal fae who fell in love with twelve royal humans. In one version, forests of silver, gold and diamond played a part."

"As it stands, all twelve of the humans have given their hearts to the fae. My sisters wish to wed their fairy lovers, and having met them all, I give my blessing."

"I see." His father frowned out the window. "If I give mine as well, what then?"

"Nothing will change, Papá. They love you and will return to you all the days of your life. Perhaps, as children come along, their visits might slow, but surely the joy of grandchildren will lessen that blow."

The king nodded slowly as if considering. "They are happy?"

"Quite. And very much in love. They will be well taken care of forever there, and treated with respect. They will be the highest of royalty and given much honor. I believe they will be happy."

"I'd like to meet these fae when I am well enough."

"I am quite certain they'd like to meet

you too." Mateo smiled, though deep down he wasn't sure it was true. Canario and the rest would be polite, he was certain, but he knew his father's blessing meant less to the fae than to his sisters.

"The young man who fell. He is your lover, I suppose?"

Mateo swallowed and nodded. "Yes. If he lives, he will be my lover."

"If he lives?"

"My sisters return to fairyland tonight to bring back more of the healing waters that saved your life and his. We didn't have much left for him, so he's fading, I'm afraid. If he makes it until morning, then he can be saved. However, the laws of fairy are such that time spent in the human world will alter him, turn him into a human, like Lámina. If he's not returned before that takes place, he'll be trapped here with us forever."

His father's rheumy eyes grew sharp and he studied Mateo. "This isn't what you wish, is it?"

"Not for him…and not for me," Mateo conceded. He didn't want to feel responsible for Ópalo's life in that way. When he'd imagined them together, it had always been in fairyland, away from his world. Their affection and intimacies had seemed a step above all that was common and grim, and it pained him to think of losing that. Less selfishly, he knew Ópalo loved his family and would want to return to his home. Mateo, at least, would be allowed to straddle the worlds, but Ópalo would be forced to give up his should the worst occur.

"Can you not take him back tonight?"

"The journey is too far. Lámina says he will die for certain if he attempts it."

"Then I pray your sisters return in time."

"Thank you." Mateo waited a few minutes, looking out the window with his father at the vast, churning sea. "Are you angry, Papá?"

"No. I am hurt your sisters did not trust me. Sad that I went to such lengths to discover the truth, only to be shut out of their lives and decisions time and again. I am ashamed that not a single one of my children thought I could be trusted with this information. I have only ever wanted what is best for all of you."

"I know, Papá. But your heart is so frail."

"My heart is not so worthless that I could not have been told of my daughters' joy or survived the surprise of discovering the unknown. As I grow old, I find I'm always on the verge of the greatest unknown there is, death. It gives me hope that there is more than I've been led to believe. Strangely, I find comfort in this new knowledge, not fear."

Mateo rubbed his face. "Papá, then why the contest?"

"When you are an old man and everything is slipping from you, you will understand desperation. Now that I know my children are happy, I can rest. I admit I went too far. And I admit…all these years I've kept you and your sisters close to me.

I've stifled you. It is no great wonder my children kept this truth from me."

"Ah, Papá, I wish they had told you sooner. I only just found out myself."

His father tried to pass him the leaves, but Mateo stayed his hand. "We needn't worry about the treasury, at least," he told his father, smiling. "My sisters can simply collect a few of these every visit and the kingdom will be wealthy for years to come."

"What of your young man, Mateo? Are you afraid for him?"

"I am, but I must admit my heart doesn't feel quite right. I care for him, and I feel I will grow to love him, but I don't understand why I feel as I do. I gave him my heart when he was dying, Lámina said it would cure him and help him live. I believe it did, but something still feels amiss. I want to know him more, and yet if he dies, I might lose that chance. If he lives I'm afraid of feeling pain like this ever again. My fear for him is great enough as it is. If I grow even fonder, his loss would be devastating."

"I understand, my dear boy, but as one who has loved greatly and lost, there is no reason to pass up joy for fear of grief. If nothing else, look what fear of grief has brought us in this debacle."

Mateo took his father's hand and kissed his knuckles. "You are wise and I will endeavor to take your words to heart, hard though it might be."

"Your heart isn't hard, my son, just cautious. That's not an unwise thing to be. Your young man waits for you, does he not? You should return to him, keep him comfortable and calm until your sisters can return. Perhaps they will bring enough water to ease the suffering of my people as well."

"We can keep some on hand, Papá. It cures all but the most dire of human ills, and for fairies it can cure almost everything except for old age and death itself."

"I see there are many blessings that will come of these unions. The greatest of which, if what you say is true, will be that I can keep your sisters near in a way that marriage to others would never allow."

"It is true, Papá, for time is quite different here than it is in fairyland."

"Tell me another day, Mateo. Your young, wounded man should not be alone while he awaits his fate."

Mateo nodded and hurried back to Ópalo with his father's blessing, one of the knots of anxiety in his gut finally unraveled.

ÓPALO TRIED TO get comfortable in the soft bed prepared for him in the study only one door down from Mateo's own room. The physician had wrapped Ópalo tightly in blankets, hoping to hold his mending bones in place, but the trip from Lámina's cottage to the comparative luxury of the castle had been excruciating anyway. Ópalo was limp with exhaustion and pain.

Ópalo was startled by Mateo holding out a shiny red apple.

"I know you cannot eat it whole quite yet, but I can feed it to you, if you'd like, in small slivers."

Ópalo smiled, or tried to. The fairy waters and his own magic were working wonders on his injuries, but the change within him, altering him quite slowly, particle by particle into a human, was a confounding countermeasure.

Mateo sat down next to him in a beautifully carved wooden chair, heavier than anything Ópalo would have designed, but fascinating all the same. He hoped to soon be well enough to take a closer look at the construction. Likewise, Mateo's knife was a cruder, heavier thing than the metal works Ópalo was accustomed to, but it didn't seem to affect Mateo's ability to slice the apple into sections so thin that they nearly dissolved when Mateo placed one on Ópalo's tongue.

The sweetness suffused his mouth, and he moaned softly. He'd eaten whatever Lámina insisted in hopes of healing faster, but everything until now had been foul medicinal herbs. The apple was heaven in comparison. "*Gracias*."

"Is it as good as you remembered?"

Ópalo laughed, but his broken ribs stabbed him and he winced. "Better."

Mateo smiled and placed another sliver in his mouth. "As good as my lips?"

"Hardly even close."

Mateo leaned forward and kissed him gently, and Ópalo sighed against his soft mouth.

"My sisters should be back in the morning with more of fairyland's waters. Do you think you can hold on until then?"

"With your tender, loving care I imagine I will survive. As to the change, my injuries seem to be working both for and against me. Returning to my home will be the best course of action to repair the damage done and restore my magic."

Mateo's eyes clouded then, and he leaned back in his chair, his hand coming up to cover his heart. "I feel no different. Rather, what I feel is so sad."

"Your heart is still your own, *mi pájaro*."

Mateo shook his head. "No, I gave it to you."

"It doesn't work quite like that. Lámina has either forgotten or is trying to trick you into feeling something you don't."

"Lámina has never lied to me."

"Then perhaps she believes you gave it, but whatever the case, Mateo, my heart feels just the same. The hole is still there. One day, I know you will fill it with your own, but that day has not come." Ópalo struggled to sit up, the pain lancing through his broken legs, but he managed. "I'm lucky indeed that the fall didn't crack my spine."

"Or your skull."

"Well, crack it very much," Ópalo said, touching the lumps that had not yet receded.

How he wished for a pond of fairy water to dip in. He'd be quite well by now.

"If my heart is still mine, then why do I feel so much despair? Seeing you this way, my own soul seems to ache."

"You might not love me just yet, Mateo, but you're a human with a kind heart, and you do care for me. That is enough to make any man feel broken. Seeing a friend, no, a lover, in the state I am in, why, you'd have to be quite cruel to not feel pain for me."

"I suppose so." Mateo rubbed his stubbly face.

"By the way, you don't have to grow that for me, though you look so dashing with it, I must say."

Mateo smirked and fed him another slice of apple. "I've been by my father's side day and night and haven't even thought of shaving." Though his eyes were still dark with sadness, he said, "I rather like having a beard. I'm told it makes me look older."

"Perhaps your sisters will finally give you

the respect you deserve."

Mateo chuckled and a spark seemed to catch for a moment inside him. Ópalo felt a corresponding easing of pain, and he smiled. "Ah, there you go. Your heart might not be mine, but mine is yours, and when you laugh, I feel better. Come, laugh some more."

"You are entirely free to be funny again."

Ópalo indicated his state. "I'm rather out of sorts at the moment, to say the least."

Mateo pressed another bite of apple between his lips and rose. "Give me a moment. I believe something helpful is in this bookcase right over here."

Ópalo noted the number of books lining one wall of the room. Mateo ran this finger over the volumes on the top shelf. "Ah. Here we go. I suppose a book of bawdy jokes will have to do?"

Ópalo settled against his pillow and smiled softly. "Please, just don't make me laugh. I only want to hear you. It's like water on stones, *mi pájaro*."

Mateo sat down next to him and said with a hint of teasing in his tone, "Then perhaps I should read silently. I'd hate to cause you more pain."

Ópalo watched as Mateo read the book, enjoying the thin slices of apple that Mateo fed him from time to time. When tears of laughter filled Mateo's eyes, Ópalo relaxed against the soft blankets, feeling slightly euphoric. The pain ebbed away almost entirely.

MATEO KNEW HE should have expected it, but he hadn't. When his sisters came through the portal armed with so many glass stoppers of fairy water that their dresses rattled as they walked, they were escorted by Canario. Mateo's father, who leaned heavily on a cane and one of the servant boys, drew himself up as best he could.

"Allow me to dispense with formalities," Canario began, after bowing over Papá's outstretched hand and kissing the knuckles perfunctorily. "But there is no time to lose if my brother is to be healed completely."

"I have done good work on him, your highness," Lámina said, bowing to Canario. "He will live and the waters will take his pain away completely."

"Lámina," Canario said, a bit of awe in his voice. "I must assure myself of my brother's state, but I wish there was time to show you the honor you are due."

"This way," Mateo said, hustling Canario out of his sisters' chambers and into the hall. The rattle behind him indicated that all eleven of his siblings followed. Ópalo was asleep, his face not nearly so swollen as even the hour before.

"Oh *pollito*," Canario murmured, stroking a hand through Ópalo's white feathers. "You are changing already." He sighed and then bent to kiss Ópalo's forehead, which roused Ópalo from his sleep.

"Canario," he gasped.

"Shh, we have the water." He turned to Mateo's sisters, who barely fit into the room.

One by one they handed their multitude of stoppered bottles to him, and Canario alternated between forcing Ópalo to drink it and pouring it directly onto his open wounds. Finally, when the last bit had been swallowed and the last wound doused, Canario sat on the bed next to Ópalo and took his hand, watching as the wounds healed before all of their eyes.

"Amazing," the king murmured. "Astounding, truly."

Canario only had eyes for Ópalo, and as his brother was finally whole, he spoke again. "What pain has our impatience wrought you? We have been so very worried. Even Halcón sends his affections."

Ópalo scoffed at that. "You needn't lie to me, brother. It appears I will live after all. Save Halcón's affection for my death bed."

Canario chuckled. "Oh, you are such a stubborn one, Ópalo. If you'd fed him cake. But no matter. Here we are, and now we must go before either of us is irrevocably lost to this world."

Mateo blinked as he realized that now Ópalo was healed, his eyebrows were beginning to molt. Soon he'd lose his feathers, and with it his fairyness.

"But the portal doesn't open again until tonight," Ópalo said, confused.

"You only need this." Canario pulled a small, dark bottle from his pocket. "Father gave it to me, and it can only be used once. I'd been saving it for an urgent situation, and I suppose this is it, *pollito*."

Ópalo sat up, Mateo's white nightshirt too big on him and slipping almost off his shoulders. He gazed behind Canario, obviously seeking someone, and Mateo thought he'd found the person when his eyes lingered on Mateo's father. "Sir," he said, nodding his head. "I wish I could stay and get to know you, but it is rather urgent that I leave. I hope you won't mind me taking this opportunity to thank you for your hospitality and to tell you that I love your son, though he does not yet love me. And I give you my solemn vow that I will only ask for his hand when I am sure he wants to share his heart with me."

Lámina made a soft noise, but didn't disagree.

Ópalo smiled at Mateo and reached out his hand. "*Mi pájaro*, I will be waiting for you."

Then Canario lifted Ópalo in his arms. Adelita opened the glass bottle, poured the black dust over both the fairies' heads, and in the cloud that rose out of it, they vanished.

Mateo rushed to the bed Ópalo had rested in and gathered handfuls of the sheets in his hand, feeling odd and bereft as his sisters crowded around him. His father took hold of his arm.

"Come, Mateo," his father said. "Let us

while away the hours before you can join him in fairyland tonight. I have much to discuss with you and your sisters. I believe there are plans to make."

Chapter Seventeen

ALTHOUGH ÓPALO WAS exhausted from all he'd experienced, when the time came to take the boats to wait for their brides, he insisted on going with his siblings. He felt sure Mateo would be with them, although doubt lingered in the corners of his mind. Of his heart.

"They're late again," Halcón muttered, but he sounded almost contrite at the same time, as if ashamed by his lack of patience. He darted a glance toward Ópalo and added, "Don't get any ideas in your head about going to fetch them, you little idiot. Just stay here and wait with the rest of us. They will come."

Ópalo coughed softly, trying to cover a smile, and dug his oar deeper into the mud at the lake bottom.

Long minutes passed until there was the sound of something dragging, and then they saw them—a tangle of brides in dresses sparkling with jewels, the king riding on a sled pulled by a large, beastly dog.

The twitters from his siblings were a rousing selection of joy, surprise and concern.

Pulse racing, Ópalo sought out Mateo's dark, curly head. When he found it, his knees strengthened and he stood upright and proud.

Mateo worked his way to the front of the group, his face lighting up when he spotted Ópalo. "You are truly healed?"

"I am. Just about." Ópalo ruffled his feathers ruefully. "My pink might not return."

"As long as you are well. That's all that matters, *mi*…" Mateo seemed to remember they were not alone. He cleared his throat and pronounced, "Our father, the king." Then he moved aside as Elisa and Gracia took one hand each to pull their father up from the sled.

The king stepped forward, his eyes narrow and his lips set in a straight line. He took them all in with a slow, serious gaze. "It is not customary in my world to take brides without asking first for their father's blessing."

Ópalo glanced down the line, and each of his siblings looked abashed.

Mateo's father continued, "However, since I have it on good authority that my daughters love each of you dearly and have promised themselves to you, I will allow your oversight to be remedied now."

Canario was the first to recover himself and quickly did as Mateo's father asked. He spoke eloquently of his love for Adelita and requested the honor of her as a bride.

The king did not make Canario wait for

his answer, instead turning to Adelita and saying, "Go now and be as happy as your mother and I once were."

Adelita fairly skipped to the boat and climbed aboard, a chaste kiss passing between her and Canario.

And so it went until the king came to Ópalo. He stared at Ópalo, saying nothing, and obviously expecting nothing. After a time, the king turned to Mateo. "If the day comes when you seek my blessing, I will give it to you."

"Thank you, Papá," Mateo said, and Ópalo felt a strange buoyancy. Mateo had not denied there was any possibility of needing his father's blessing.

"My daughters will return to me every day until I am gone from the earth," the king went on in a commanding voice. "Vow it."

Ópalo and his siblings answered in unison. "You have our word."

"Childbed or illness will be the only exception."

When Canario bowed and thanked the king for his leniency, Ópalo's siblings took note and bowed as well.

Mateo walked toward his father. "You grow tired, Father. I think it is time you go home."

"Indeed."

"I shall walk Papá back to the portal," Mateo said. "Ópalo, if you are willing to wait longer, I can return."

"No, my favorite boy, run along with your lover," his father said. "I can make it back safely."

The king called the great dog to him and climbed aboard the sleigh. "Breakfast will be early, my darlings," the king said in a tired voice. "Sleep well."

With a bark the dog set off, and they were gone.

MATEO'S BODY WAS warm underneath his as they lay at the bottom of the boat alongside the oars. A rose stem had been left behind, failing to make it overboard with the rest, and Mateo was still bleeding a bit on his bearded cheek where it had scratched him. Ópalo ran his thumb over the cut and wiped away the bright-red. Then he leaned over the edge, dipped his hand in the water and brought a wet finger to the cut. He smiled as the wound began to heal immediately.

"I have missed this," Mateo said, reaching down to squeeze Ópalo's ass. "When I saw you there, broken on the cobblestones, I feared, oh, I was quite numb with fear, actually. I thought I'd never know you or see you again."

"Fairies are stronger than we look," Ópalo said.

"You don't have to convince me. The miracles I witnessed with my own eyes cannot be overstated."

Mateo gripped him closer and they

began to move together again. The boat rocked on the waves of the lake in the rhythm of their lust, and Mateo whimpered in urgent frustration.

"What is it?"

"I only wish the boat was big enough for you to fuck me properly. I long for your cock inside me, Ópalo. I long for so much."

Still they rutted against each other, prick against prick, mouths pressed urgently together, cries rising as they reached another climax and wet spurts of seed pulsed between their shaking bodies.

His heart pounding and Mateo's panting breath tickling his ear, Ópalo snuggled in closer. Who needed dancing when they had this? The stars above were faint, but the moon was wide and brilliant, illuminating them in glossy, opalescent light.

"What did you think of our world?" Mateo asked when his breath had slowed again.

"It was quite dark, and everything

seemed very small. I regret that I can never stay long enough to explore it fully."

"I am so grateful that Canario saved you as he did." Mateo brushed his hair over Ópalo's feathers. "I rather like the white. It suits you."

"Does it? For that at least, I'm glad." Ópalo kissed Mateo's neck. "Lámina is not what I expected her to be. After all the stories of her sacrifice, I thought she would be regal and stately. More like Blanca."

"Ah yes, Lámina is quite odd."

"I have to agree," Ópalo said. "I mean no insult to your world, but I would not want to give up my home to stay there."

"I love it, but it seems quite changed in my eyes now that I've been here. Though, for now, *mi pájaro*, I still choose not to eat."

"The food is not that delicious anyway," Ópalo teased.

In the quiet of the night, they rested together. Ópalo kissed the edge of Mateo's mouth and settled down, resting his head against Mateo's chest. He listened to the sound of Mateo's human heart. He closed his eyes, soaking it in.

It wasn't his yet, but one day it would be.

Epilogue

"ONCE UPON A time, in a kingdom by the great, foamy sea," Mateo began, kneeling down to speak to the children who stared up him with rapt expressions. "There lived a kind human king and his wonderful human queen. Over the years, they were blessed with eleven human princesses, each more beautiful than the last."

"That's my mama," Luz's eldest girl, Colorista, chirped.

"And one incredibly, devastatingly handsome human prince."

His little nieces and nephews twittered with excitement, their feathers fluffing. They loved the part of the story set in the human world the most, and it amused him to think of his own childhood seated in Lámina's lap, listening to her speak of her world as if it was a fantasy land.

"Do they never tire of this one?" Ópalo asked good-naturedly. He leaned against a tall pole on the side of the dock, looking fanciful in his newest breeches, dyed with some berry that made them a bright purple. The color set off his white feathers.

"No, Uncle!" Flora cried, her yellow feathers bristling at him. Her concern that Mateo might not finish the tale marred her pretty features. "Don't take him away yet. The story isn't over!"

Mateo smirked. He too would like to rush off to their nest, but the children had taken to greeting him at the dock when he arrived, along with the flocks of cousins.

"Then let me have the honor of finishing it for him," Ópalo said, grinning. A sigh went through the children. They knew story time was about to be cut short. "All eleven human princesses and one charming human prince came to fairyland, fell in love and everyone but the incredibly handsome human prince and the famously attractive youngest fairy prince had elaborate weddings with all the best food and lived happily ever after with a lot of squalling babies who grew up to be adorable little fae who loved their uncles dearly and understood that after three days apart they wanted to be alone together. The end."

"Only one day for him," Marvolo mumbled with an expression quite like Imelda.

For a moment Mateo thought they might argue, but they didn't. One by one they hugged him and scampered off in a dazzling show of feathers and color. Mateo watched, amused and now happily alone with Ópalo.

Ópalo grinned. "I think you should take your famously attractive fairy prince back to our nest." He held out his hand.

"Famously?" Mateo laughed.

"Of course."

Mateo gazed down at Ópalo's face, taking in the blue eyes, the feathers and soft lips he'd kissed so often. "How many years have I been coming here now?"

"In your world's calculations or mine?" Ópalo asked, and his brow furrowed, obviously attempting to do the math in his head.

Mateo cut off his efforts with a kiss. "It doesn't matter. Yes, let's go home."

Ópalo launched out in front of him, striding with great purpose, before turning around and calling, "Race you!"

"Wait! Let us go by the dance and grab some wine. There'll be cakes. Your favorites."

Ópalo shook his head, his backward steps speeding up, clearly trying to get a head start to win.

Mateo remembered the night his father had died, and how the three days with Ópalo had steadied him for the grim reality of the service and the responsibilities of the throne. He remembered long nights of laughter, and the first time he saw Ópalo dancing playfully with Adelita's little boy. He remembered the fights they had over stupid things like whether to ride horses or swim in the lake. He thought of the way Ópalo smelled like wood dust after working on a project and still looked like the most delicious cake ever made.

Over the years, so much had changed. Yet one thing had not changed at all, only growing stronger and more real, until it had become the most real thing of all.

"Come," Ópalo called again, still trying to get Mateo to run after him.

"No! Let's get cakes!"

"I'm not hungry for cakes!"

Mateo ran then, chased Ópalo across the green grass toward the entrance that led most quickly to their rooms. He grabbed him next to the roses and kissed his mouth hard. Ópalo laughed, and returned his urgency before breaking away and tugging at his hand, clearly eager to be alone. But Mateo did not budge.

"Ópalo, I'm ready," Mateo said.

"So am I, my stubborn bird! Why are you dragging your feet?" he grinned and lifted his brows in a hilarious attempt at lechery. Mateo pulled him close, lifted his chin and gazed down into his eyes. He waited until Ópalo stopped laughing and grew serious.

"What's wrong?"

"I want to go by the dance, because I wish to eat cake, *mi pájaro*."

Mateo watched Ópalo's face explode with delight and ecstatic joy. If he'd thought his declaration would result in a detour by the dance so he might declare his love publicly and take a wedding vow in the form of a piece of fairy cake washed down with wine, he was mistaken.

It wasn't until two hours later, after Ópalo had proven again how strong he was by hauling Mateo up to their nest and stripping his clothes in such a way that they were left in ruins, and after Ópalo had buggered him and they were covered in spendings, sweat and feathers, that Mateo even had a chance to express his disappointment in not getting to experience the aphrodisiac of the cake before their coupling.

Ópalo, tucked into the slot between Mateo's arm and his body, slapped Mateo's chest with the back of his hand. "The cake is rather tasteless anyway," Ópalo said. "And our pleasure can't be very much greater than it is."

Mateo scoffed. "It's as though you don't want me to have it."

Ópalo looked vaguely embarrassed. "I like knowing that you've chosen me. The hole in my heart has long been filled, *mi pájaro*. It stopped aching years ago."

"Then what was all this for?" Mateo asked gesturing between them at the evidence of Ópalo's enthusiasm at Mateo's declaration of intent toward the fairy cake.

"You love me."

Mateo touched Ópalo's face tenderly. "I do love you. Lámina was right. I gave you my heart long ago before I could admit it to myself. It is how it is and always will be."

THE END

"I loved this book. Really LOVED it. The author once again proves her extraordinary versatility. This book is so much more than a love story. So multi-layered. So wonderful."

– Katerina, Don't Love Me, Jack Reviews

"[Alpha/Omega] isn't everybody's cuppa, I can't say this book will be for everyone, but I can say that Slow Heat is some of the best I've read yet."

– Lisa, The Novel Approach

A lustful young alpha meets his match in an older omega with a past.

Professor Vale Aman has crafted a good life for himself. An unbonded omega in his mid-thirties, he's long since given up hope that he'll meet a compatible alpha, let alone his destined mate. He's fulfilled by his career, his poetry, his cat, and his friends.

When Jason Sabel, a much younger alpha, imprints on Vale in a shocking and public way, longings are ignited that can't be ignored. Fighting their strong sexual urges, Jason and Vale must agree to contract with each other before they can consummate their passion.

But for Vale, being with Jason means giving up his independence and placing his future in the hands of an untested alpha—as well as facing the scars of his own tumultuous past. He isn't sure it's worth it. But Jason isn't giving up his destined mate without a fight.

This is a stand-alone gay romance novel, 118,000 words, with a strong HFN ending, as well as a well-crafted, non-shifter omegaverse, with alphas, betas, omegas, male pregnancy, heat, and knotting. Content warning for pregnancy loss and aftermath.

HEAT FOR SALE

Omegaverse with knotting, heat, and pregnancy!
Erotic with interesting world-building!
Older alpha, younger omega!

"This book is as hot as the proverbial fires of hell."

– Mirrigold Reviews.

Heat can be sold but love is earned.

In a world where omegas sell their heats for profit, Adrien is a university student in need of funding. With no family to fall back on, he reluctantly allows the university's matcher to offer his virgin heat for auction online. Anxious, but aware this is the reality of life for all omegas, Adrien hopes whoever wins his heat will be kind.

Heath—a wealthy, older alpha—is rocked by the young man's resemblance to his dead lover, Nathan. When Heath discovers Adrien is Nathan's lost son from his first heat years before they met, he becomes obsessed with the idea of reclaiming a piece of Nathan.

Heath buys Adrien's heat with only one motivation: to impregnate Adrien, claim the child, and move on. But their undeniable passion shocks him. Adrien doesn't know what to make of the handsome, mysterious stranger he's pledged his body to, but he's soon swept away in the heat of the moment and surrenders to Heath entirely.

Once Adrien is pregnant, Heath secrets him away to his immense and secluded home. As the birth draws near, Heath grows to love Adrien for the man he is, not just for his connection to Nathan. Unaware of Heath's past with his omega parent and coming to depend on him, heart and soul, Adrien begins to fall as well.

But as their love blossoms, Nathan's shadow looms. Can Heath keep his new love and the child they've made together once

Adrien discovers his secrets?

Heat for Sale is a stand-alone m/m erotic romance by Leta Blake. Infused with a du Maurier Rebecca-style secret, it features a well-realized omegaverse, an age-gap, dominance and submission, heats, knotting, and scorching hot scenes.

OMEGA MINE:
The Search for a Soulmate

Grumpy, oblivious bear shifter finally
recognizes his sweet, destined mate!

Opposites attract! Shifter universe!

Short Novel Length

**Can an Alpha find his dream Omega on
reality TV?**

Alpha Hank Morrow is a police officer
and Alpha bear shifter who has never found
the right Omega. Without the steadying
influence of a bond with his Omega, Hank's
powerful Alpha senses are beginning to
overwhelm and endanger not only him, but
his fellow police officers and the entire city of
White Edge. The chief of police and the
governor sign Hank up for a reality TV show
to help unmatched Alphas find their dream
Omega.

Omega Mine: Search for a Soulmate certainly isn't Hank's idea of a great plan, but

he's not given a choice. Now he's off to a tropical island to meet over one hundred potential Omegas in a televised version of hell.

Or is it?

Evan Vaughn is an unmatched Omega. He and Hank have actually met once before at an Alpha-Omega mixer, but apparently he didn't make much of an impression at the time. Will that change on the set of *Omega Mine*? And can anything real come out of a reality TV dating show? Hank and Evan are about to find out…

The Bachelor **meets Alpha-Omega romance!**

This book is nearly 40,000 words of an oblivious bear shifter finally meeting his soul bonded match and a happy ending you'll love! Warning: There is no mfm in this book. There is no ménage in this book. There is no cheating in this book. There is an attraction to someone that is not the other MC but it does not come to fruition.

Other Books by Leta Blake

Contemporary

Will & Patrick Wake Up Married
Will & Patrick's Endless Honeymoon
Cowboy Seeks Husband
The Difference Between
Bring on Forever
Stay Lucky

Sports

The River Leith

The Training Season Series
Training Season
Training Complex

Musicians

Smoky Mountain Dreams
Vespertine

New Adult

Punching the V-Card

'90s Coming of Age Series
Pictures of You
You Are Not Me
Only You

Winter Holidays

North's Pole

The Mr. Christmas Series
Mr. Frosty Pants
Mr. Naughty List
Mr. Jingle Bells

A Boy for All Seasons
My December Daddy

Fantasy

Any Given Lifetime

Reimagined Fairy Tales

Flight
Levity

Paranormal & Shifters

Angel Undone
Omega Mine

Horror

Raise Up Heart

Omegaverse

Heat of Love Series
White Heat
Slow Heat

Alpha Heat
Slow Birth
Bitter Heat

For Sale Series
Heat for Sale
Bully for Sale

Audiobooks
letablake.com/audiobooks

Discover more about the author online

Leta Blake
letablake.com

Gay Romance Newsletter

Leta's newsletter will keep you up to date on her latest releases, sales and deals, future writing plans, and more from the world of M/M romance. Join Leta's mailing list today.

Leta Blake on Patreon

Become part of Leta Blake's Patreon community to support her indie publishing expenses and to access exclusive content, deleted scenes, extras, and interviews.

Author of the bestselling book *Smoky Mountain Dreams* and fan favorites like *Training Season*, *Will & Patrick Wake Up Married*, and *Slow Heat*, Leta Blake has been captivating M/M Romance readers for over a decade. Whether writing contemporary romance or fantasy, she puts her psychology background to use creating complex characters and love stories that feel real. At home in the Southern U.S., Leta works hard at achieving balance between her writing and her family life.